This Walker book belongs to:

_____

_____

_____

Hail, Reader!

I am DORMEO, a dormouse, gladiator, berry nibbler and your guide to ancient Rome. My ancestors have lived on the Palatine Hill since the time of Romulus and Remus. In fact, one of my relations was actually eaten by the she-wolf who adopted those wild twins! My family have witnessed the rise and fall of Rome. We have also had the terrifying honour of being a favourite food of the Romans – many's the time that the only thing between me and a Roman's digestive juices was my gladiator's helmet, so I won't be taking that off, even for you! However, I will tell you everything you need to know about the ups and downs of life in Rome. Just keep me supplied with berries or I might ... yawn ... be forced ... yawn ... to hibernate ... large yawn ... before you have finished reading.

Semper vale et salve,

Dormeo Augustus

PS – semper vale et salve means "best wishes" in Latin, which is the language of all good Romans.

PPS – this letter is written on a scrap of scroll I rescued from the city of Rome as it fell about my twitching whiskers!

PPPS – snore...

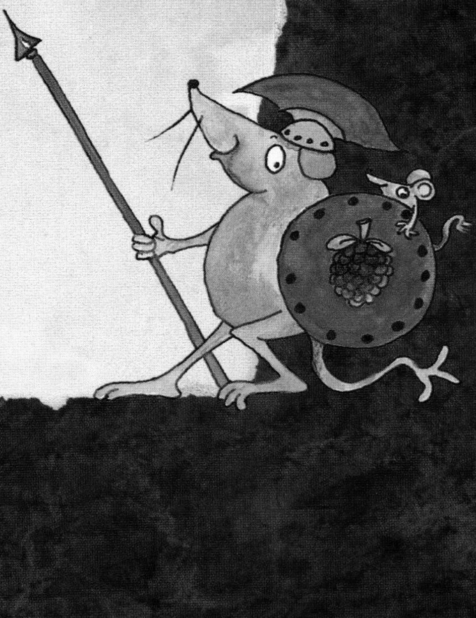

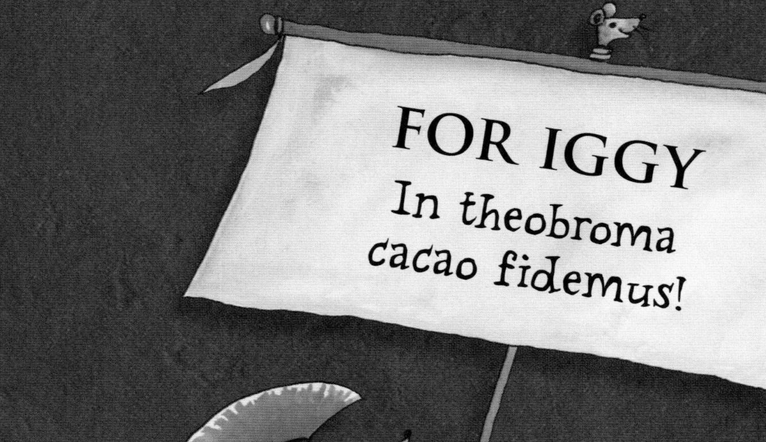
FOR IGGY
In theobroma cacao fidemus!

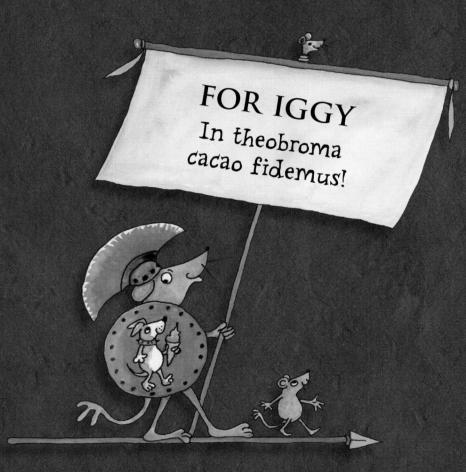

THE ROMANS
GODS · EMPERORS
· AND DORMICE ·

Written and illustrated by
MARCIA WILLIAMS

WALKER BOOKS
AND SUBSIDIARIES
LONDON · BOSTON · SYDNEY · AUCKLAND

FROM MUDDLE TO MANKIND!

Follow your guide. That's me, Dormeo!

The Romans borrowed many myths.

They also borrowed gods and spirits – mostly from the Greeks!

Res vera means "true fact" in Latin.

Am I up or down?

Should I be awake ...

... or asleep?

In the beginning the world was a great big muddle.

I need to know where I am!

Then a god decided to sort the whole mess out.

You there and you there!

He divided night from day and the land from the sea and sky.

One for Moon. One for Sun.

He also created a myriad of creatures and plants.

It's fine for you, up in the clouds, but I need some friends down here.

Well, you create them; it's my rest day!

Most of his relations were really impressed. Only Prometheus was disappointed.
He was lonely and wanted a few playmates.

RES VERA
The Romans believed that humans are special as they stand up straight with their
eyes turned towards the stars. Other creatures hang their heads towards the ground.

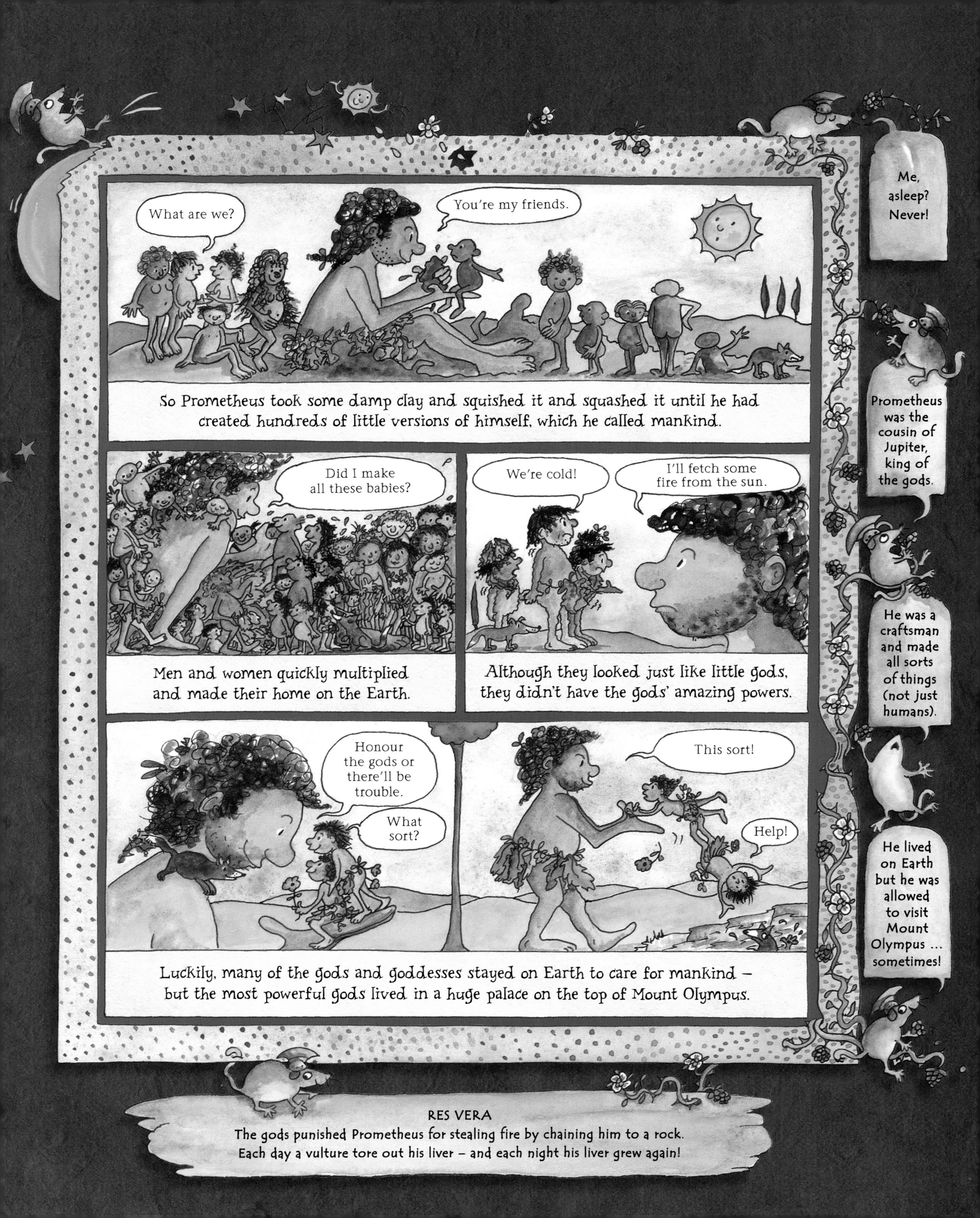
What are we?
You're my friends.
So Prometheus took some damp clay and squished it and squashed it until he had created hundreds of little versions of himself, which he called mankind.
Did I make all these babies?
Men and women quickly multiplied and made their home on the Earth.
We're cold!
I'll fetch some fire from the sun.
Although they looked just like little gods, they didn't have the gods' amazing powers.
Honour the gods or there'll be trouble.
What sort?
This sort!
Help!
Luckily, many of the gods and goddesses stayed on Earth to care for mankind – but the most powerful gods lived in a huge palace on the top of Mount Olympus.
Me, asleep? Never!
Prometheus was the cousin of Jupiter, king of the gods.
He was a craftsman and made all sorts of things (not just humans).
He lived on Earth but he was allowed to visit Mount Olympus … sometimes!

RES VERA

The gods punished Prometheus for stealing fire by chaining him to a rock. Each day a vulture tore out his liver – and each night his liver grew again!

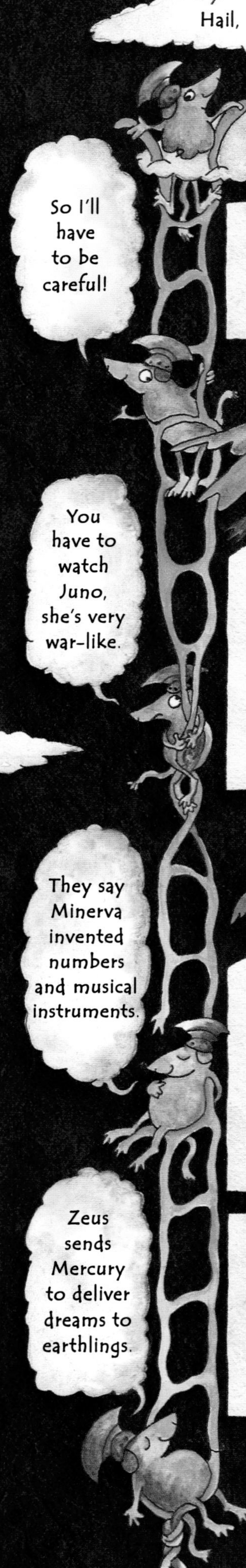
Hail, Reader! The gods don't like visitors.
So I'll have to be careful!
You have to watch Juno, she's very war-like.
They say Minerva invented numbers and musical instruments.
Zeus sends Mercury to deliver dreams to earthlings.

THE GODS AND GODDESSES ...

The people Prometheus created had to keep the twelve most powerful gods on Mount Olympus happy – otherwise the gods wouldn't keep them safe. They built temples in the gods' honour and chose priests and priestesses to organize their festivals and sacrifices. You ignored the Olympic gods at your peril, for they were quick to anger and slow to forgive!

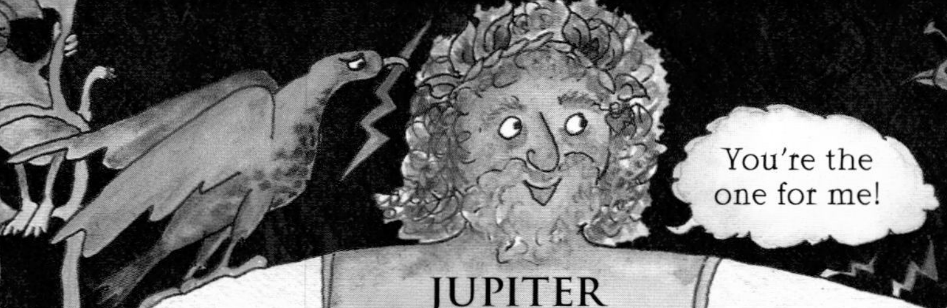
You're the one for me!

JUPITER

The god of the sky, thunder, lightning and the king of all the gods, Jupiter helped people stay on the path of honour and duty. If he was upset, he would throw lightning bolts! Jupiter's wife, Juno, was very fiery – even Jupiter was scared of her. Luckily he could change himself into an animal and hide from her.

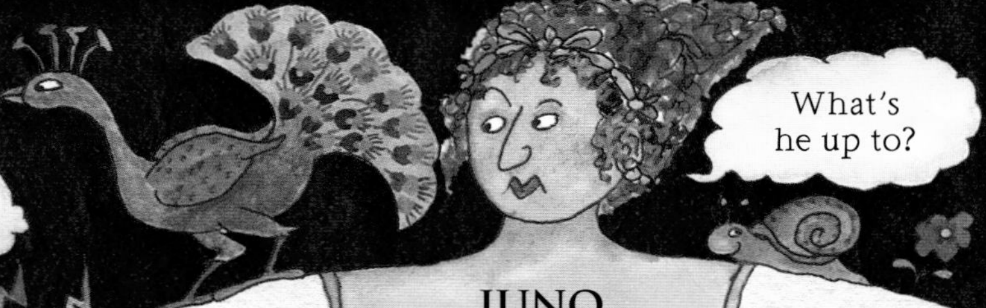
What's he up to?

JUNO

Juno was the queen of the gods, goddess of women and marriage. Juno was youthful, lively, strong and jealous. She had an amazing bodyguard, Argus, who had a hundred eyes. Juno was Jupiter's sister as well as his wife, and she had two children, Mars and Vulcan.

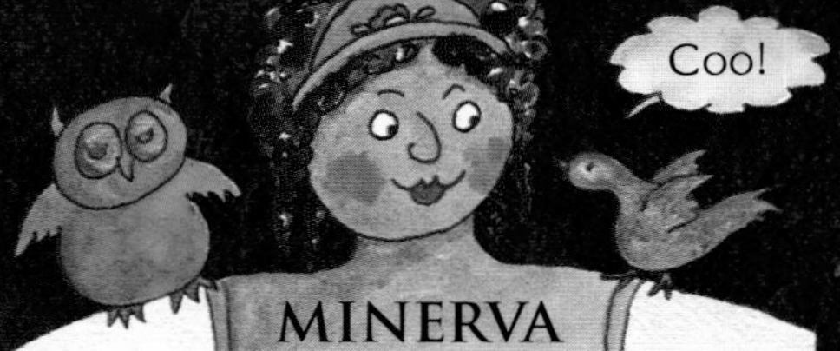
Coo!

MINERVA

Minerva was the goddess of wisdom and Jupiter's favourite daughter. She was born from his brain and was both beautiful and powerful. Juno hated her.

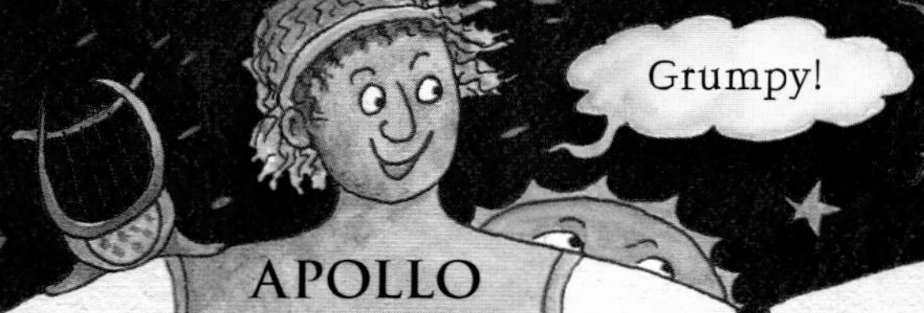
Grumpy!

APOLLO

Another of Jupiter's children, Apollo was the god of the sun, music, healing and prophecy. He was warm-hearted and popular. Wherever he went, sunshine and music followed in his path.

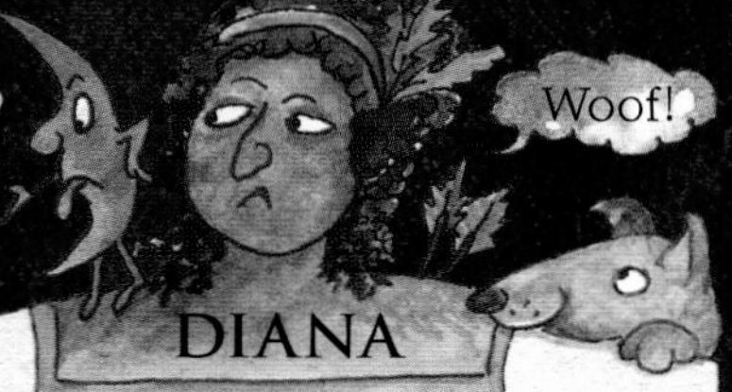
Woof!

DIANA

The twin sister of Apollo and goddess of the moon and hunting. Diana could talk to animals and make them obey her. Unlike Apollo, Diana was cold-hearted and only loved her dogs.

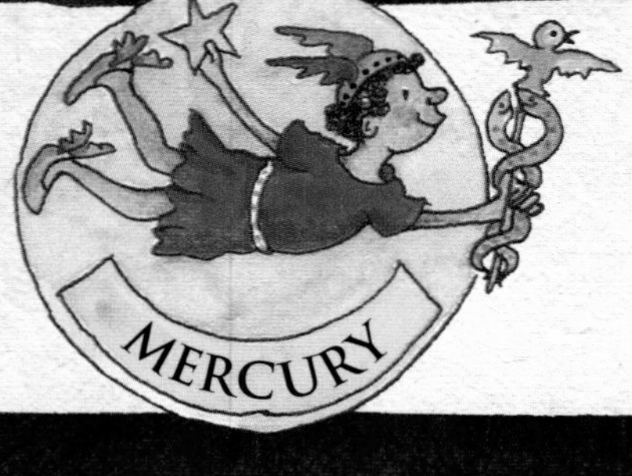
MERCURY

Jupiter's youngest son and a firm favourite with the Romans, Mercury was born with a twinkle in his eye and grew up to be clever and very speedy, so Jupiter made him the messenger to the gods. All the gods and goddesses trusted Mercury with their secrets!

RES VERA

As Rome expanded, the number of gods also grew. The Romans adopted new gods from the places they invaded.

… OF MOUNT OLYMPUS

The Roman people loved their gods, goddesses and spirits. They saw them in flowers, in streams, on door latches, even under their beds. There were special gods to protect you in the countryside and public shrines to honour them, and each home had a shrine in honour of the household gods. Vesta, the goddess of fire, was worshipped in every home.

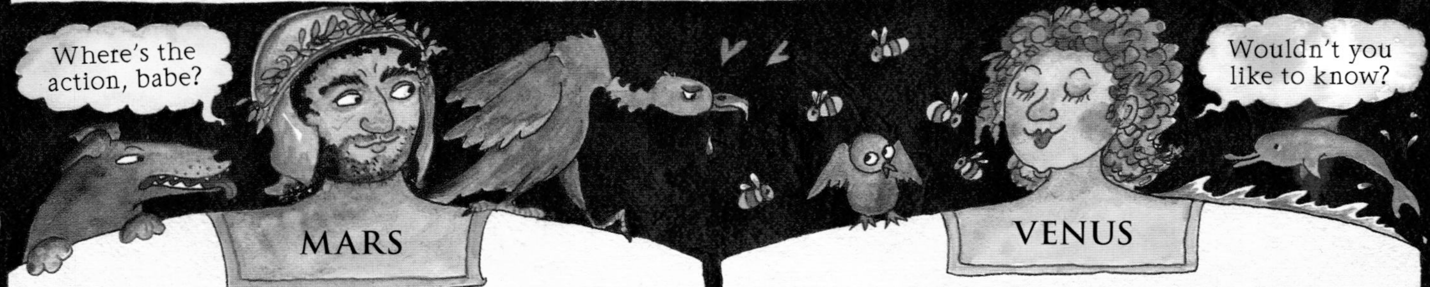

Where's the action, babe?
Wouldn't you like to know?

MARS

The most important god after Jupiter, Mars was the god of war, nature, spring and cattle. He was the son of Juno and a magic flower! Mars was a handsome, vain troublemaker who loved battles and bloodshed. The other gods tried to avoid him and his sidekick, Discordia, who was the spirit of disagreement.

VENUS

The goddess of love, vegetation and beauty, Venus was dear to every Roman's heart. She was born from sea foam and rose up from the sea on a shell as a fully-grown woman. Venus married Vulcan, but she hated being tied to him. She was always on the lookout, amongst both gods and mortals, for a more exciting love.

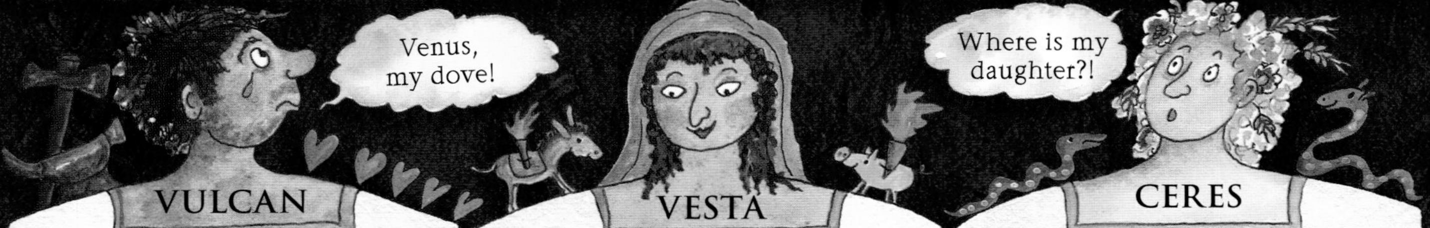

Venus, my dove!
Where is my daughter?!

VULCAN

Vulcan was the god of fire and forge. If he stoked his furnaces too hard volcanoes erupted! He adored Venus, even though she mistreated him. He was the son of Jupiter and Juno and he was born with a limp.

VESTA

The goddess of the hearth and home, Vesta was sister to Jupiter and Juno. Unlike her siblings she was kind and watched over women, who honoured her by throwing cakes into their fires.

CERES

The goddess of the harvest, Ceres was Jupiter's third sister. If she was upset then crops failed and people starved. When her daughter, Proserpina, vanished, the fields became deserts until she was found.

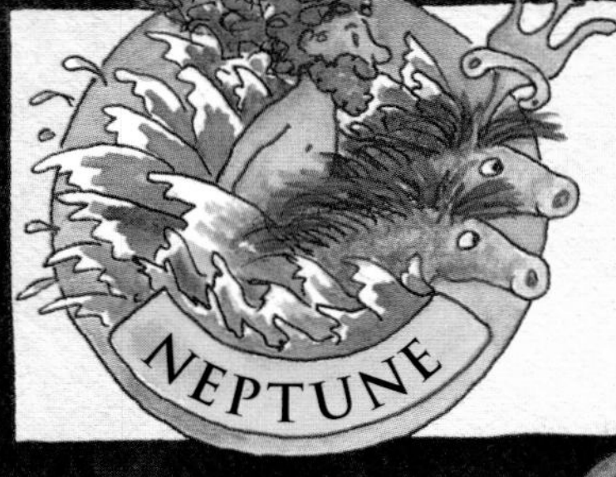

NEPTUNE

The god of the sea and fresh water, Neptune was the brother of Jupiter and Dis, the god of the underworld. He was powerful, moody and very good-looking, with green hair and blue eyes. He only visited Mount Olympus occasionally, as he preferred to ride his horses through the waves.

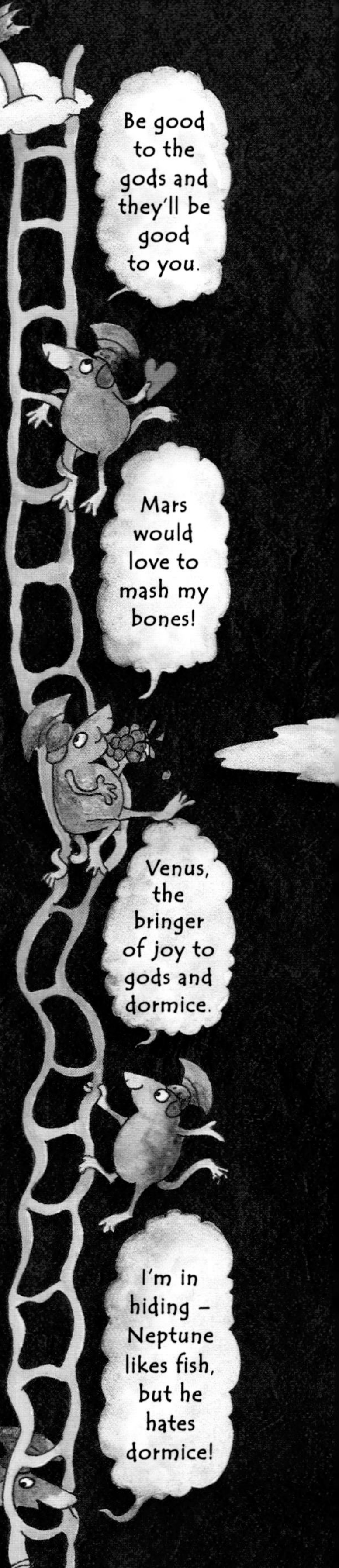

Be good to the gods and they'll be good to you.
Mars would love to mash my bones!
Venus, the bringer of joy to gods and dormice.
I'm in hiding – Neptune likes fish, but he hates dormice!

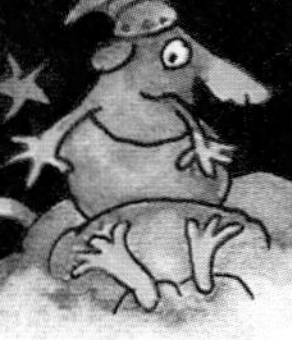

RES VERA
The goddess of Rome was Roma.
Her image appeared on early Roman coins.

THE BIRTH OF ROMULUS AND REMUS

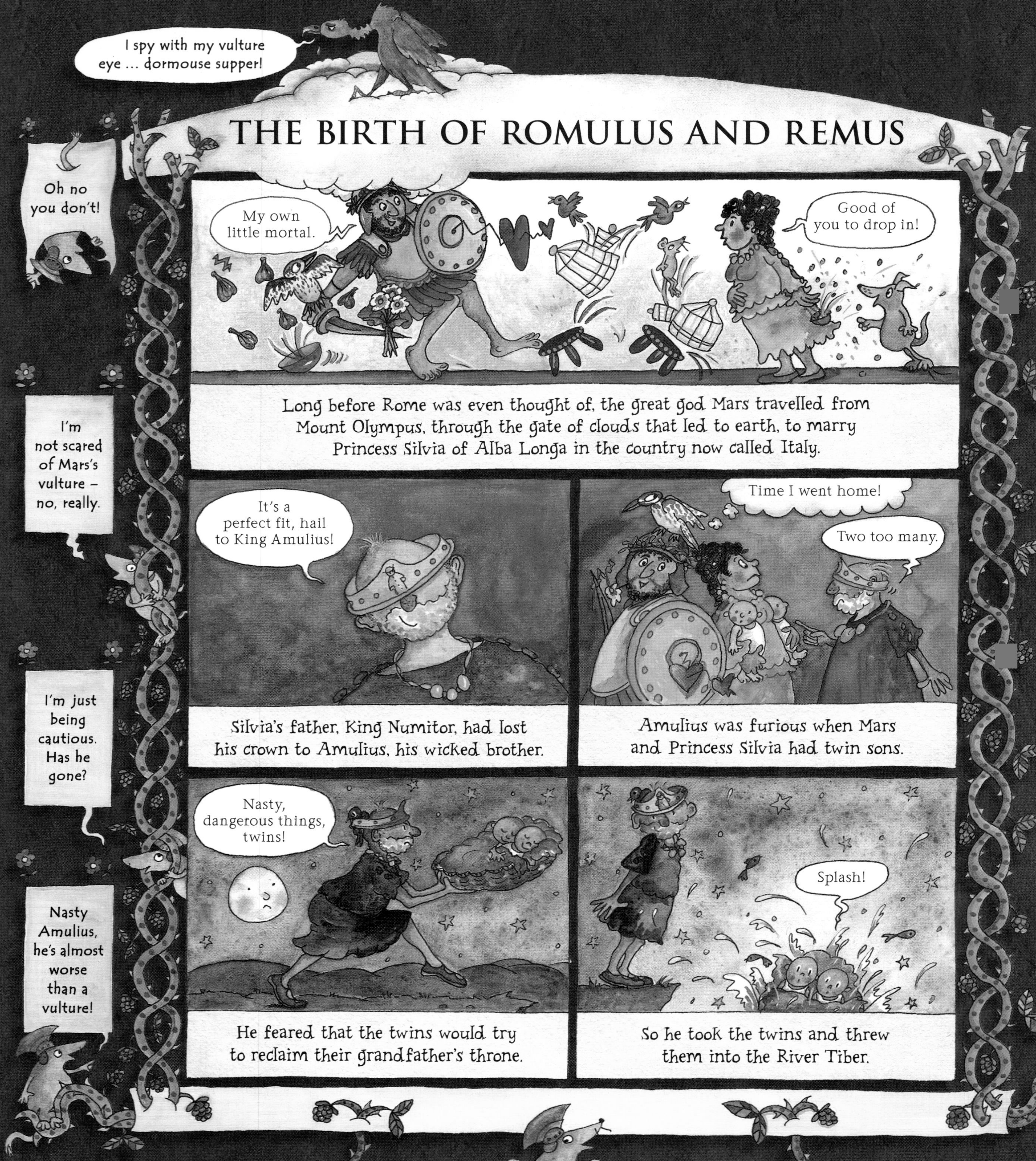

I spy with my vulture eye ... dormouse supper!
Oh no you don't!
My own little mortal.
Good of you to drop in!
I'm not scared of Mars's vulture – no, really.
It's a perfect fit, hail to King Amulius!
Time I went home!
Two too many.
I'm just being cautious. Has he gone?
Nasty, dangerous things, twins!
Splash!
Nasty Amulius, he's almost worse than a vulture!

Long before Rome was even thought of, the great god Mars travelled from Mount Olympus, through the gate of clouds that led to earth, to marry Princess Silvia of Alba Longa in the country now called Italy.

Silvia's father, King Numitor, had lost his crown to Amulius, his wicked brother.

Amulius was furious when Mars and Princess Silvia had twin sons.

He feared that the twins would try to reclaim their grandfather's throne.

So he took the twins and threw them into the River Tiber.

RES VERA

Some say that after the birth of the twins, Amulius buried Silvia alive. She was rescued by the river god Tiberinus, who later married her.

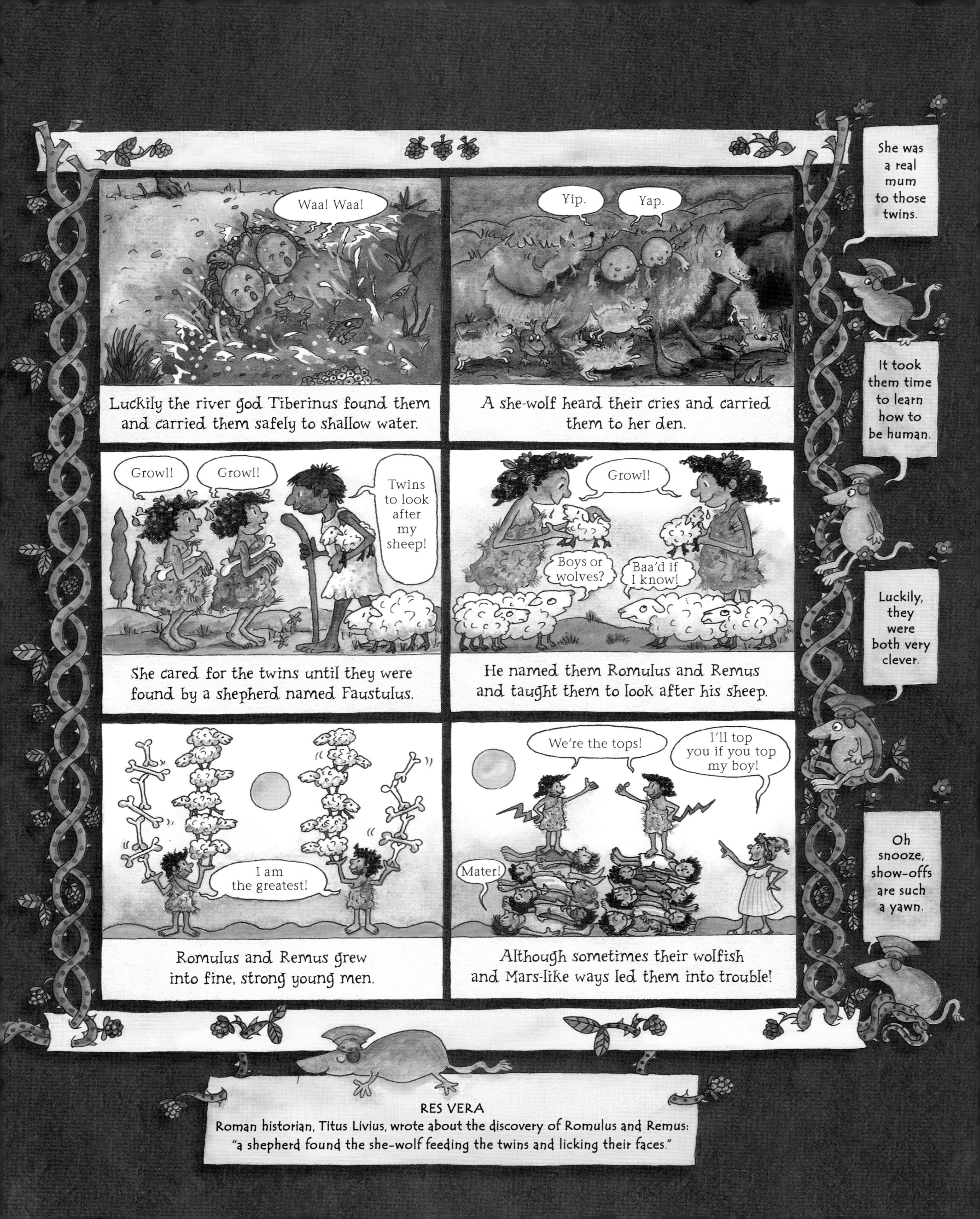
Waa! Waa!
Luckily the river god Tiberinus found them and carried them safely to shallow water.
Yip.
Yap.
A she-wolf heard their cries and carried them to her den.
She was a real mum to those twins.
Growl!
Growl!
Twins to look after my sheep!
She cared for the twins until they were found by a shepherd named Faustulus.
Growl!
Boys or wolves?
Baa'd if I know!
He named them Romulus and Remus and taught them to look after his sheep.
It took them time to learn how to be human.
Luckily, they were both very clever.
I am the greatest!
Romulus and Remus grew into fine, strong young men.
We're the tops!
I'll top you if you top my boy!
Mater!
Although sometimes their wolfish and Mars-like ways led them into trouble!
Oh snooze, show-offs are such a yawn.

RES VERA

Roman historian, Titus Livius, wrote about the discovery of Romulus and Remus: "a shepherd found the she-wolf feeding the twins and licking their faces."

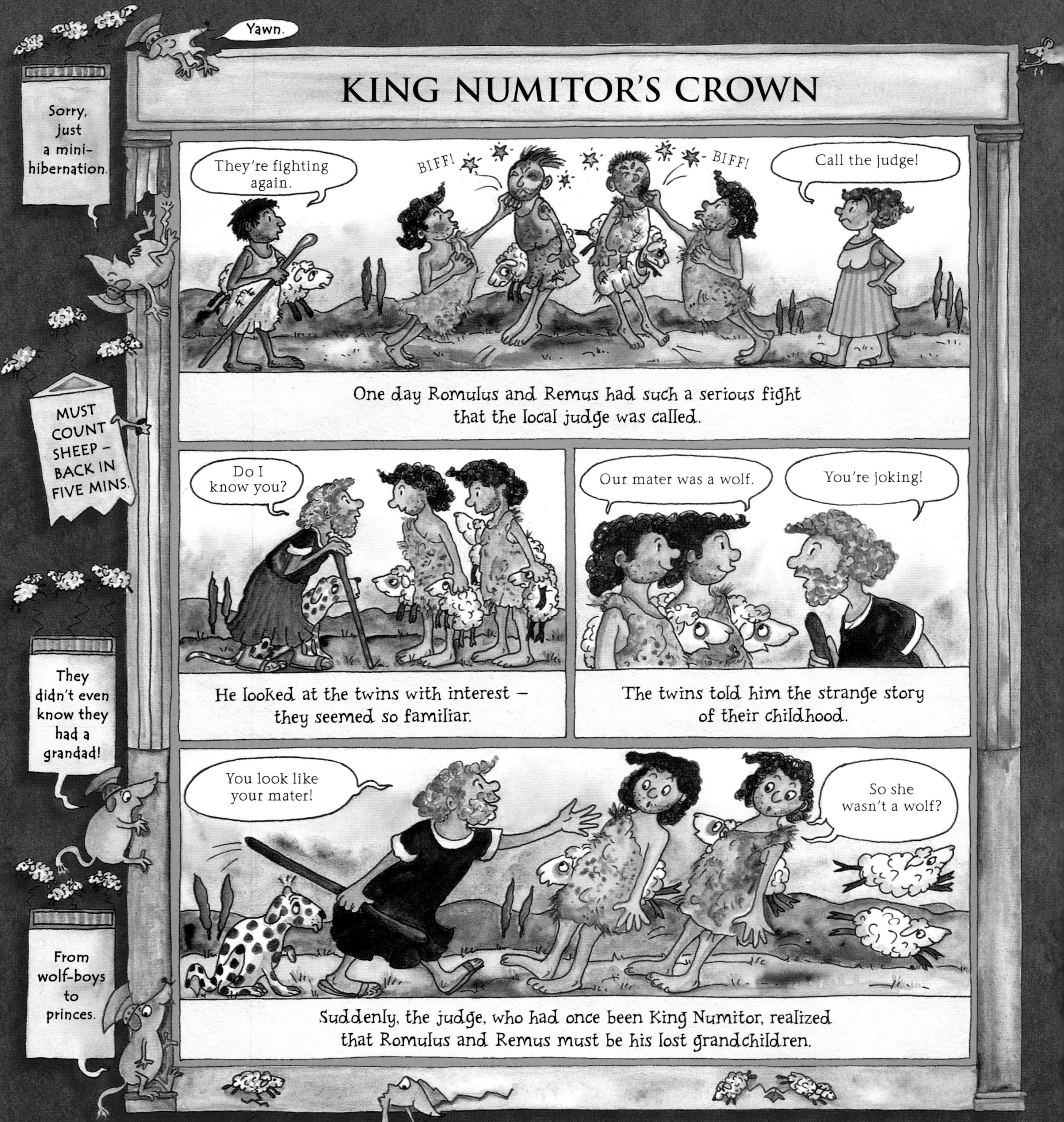
Yawn.
KING NUMITOR'S CROWN
Sorry, just a mini-hibernation.
They're fighting again.
BIFF!
BIFF!
Call the judge!
One day Romulus and Remus had such a serious fight that the local judge was called.
MUST COUNT SHEEP – BACK IN FIVE MINS.
Do I know you?
He looked at the twins with interest – they seemed so familiar.
Our mater was a wolf.
You're joking!
The twins told him the strange story of their childhood.
They didn't even know they had a grandad!
You look like your mater!
So she wasn't a wolf?
Suddenly, the judge, who had once been King Numitor, realized that Romulus and Remus must be his lost grandchildren.
From wolf-boys to princes.

RES VERA

It is believed that a woodpecker helped the she-wolf feed the twins. The wolf and the woodpecker are both sacred animals of Mars.

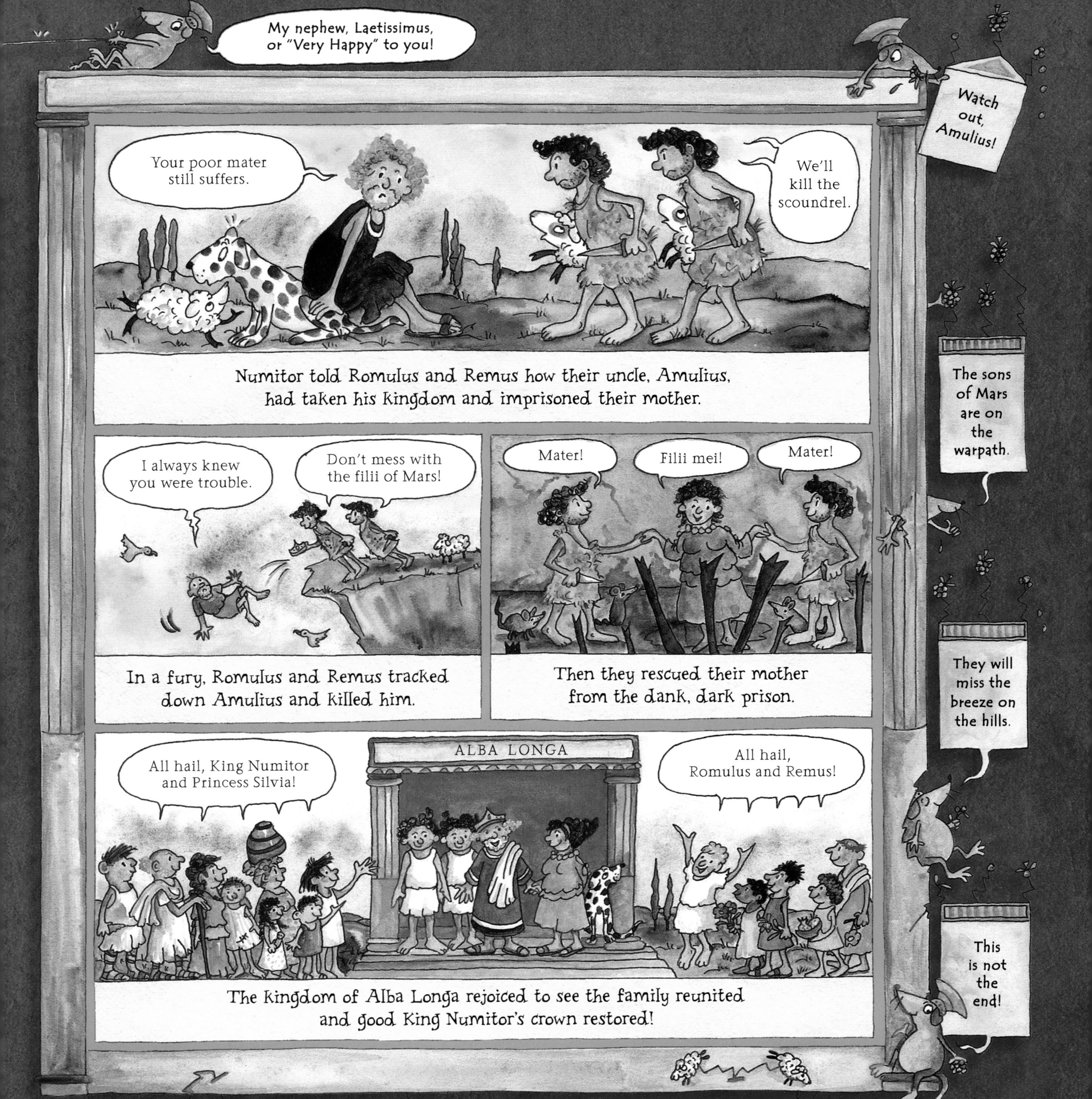
My nephew, Laetissimus, or "Very Happy" to you!
Watch out, Amulius!
Your poor mater still suffers.
We'll kill the scoundrel.
Numitor told Romulus and Remus how their uncle, Amulius, had taken his kingdom and imprisoned their mother.
The sons of Mars are on the warpath.
I always knew you were trouble.
Don't mess with the filii of Mars!
In a fury, Romulus and Remus tracked down Amulius and killed him.
Mater!
Filii mei!
Mater!
Then they rescued their mother from the dank, dark prison.
They will miss the breeze on the hills.
ALBA LONGA
All hail, King Numitor and Princess Silvia!
All hail, Romulus and Remus!
The kingdom of Alba Longa rejoiced to see the family reunited and good King Numitor's crown restored!
This is not the end!

RES VERA

The kingdom of Alba Longa was in a part of Italy called Latium. The Latin tribe had settled there as the land was close to the River Tiber and very fertile.

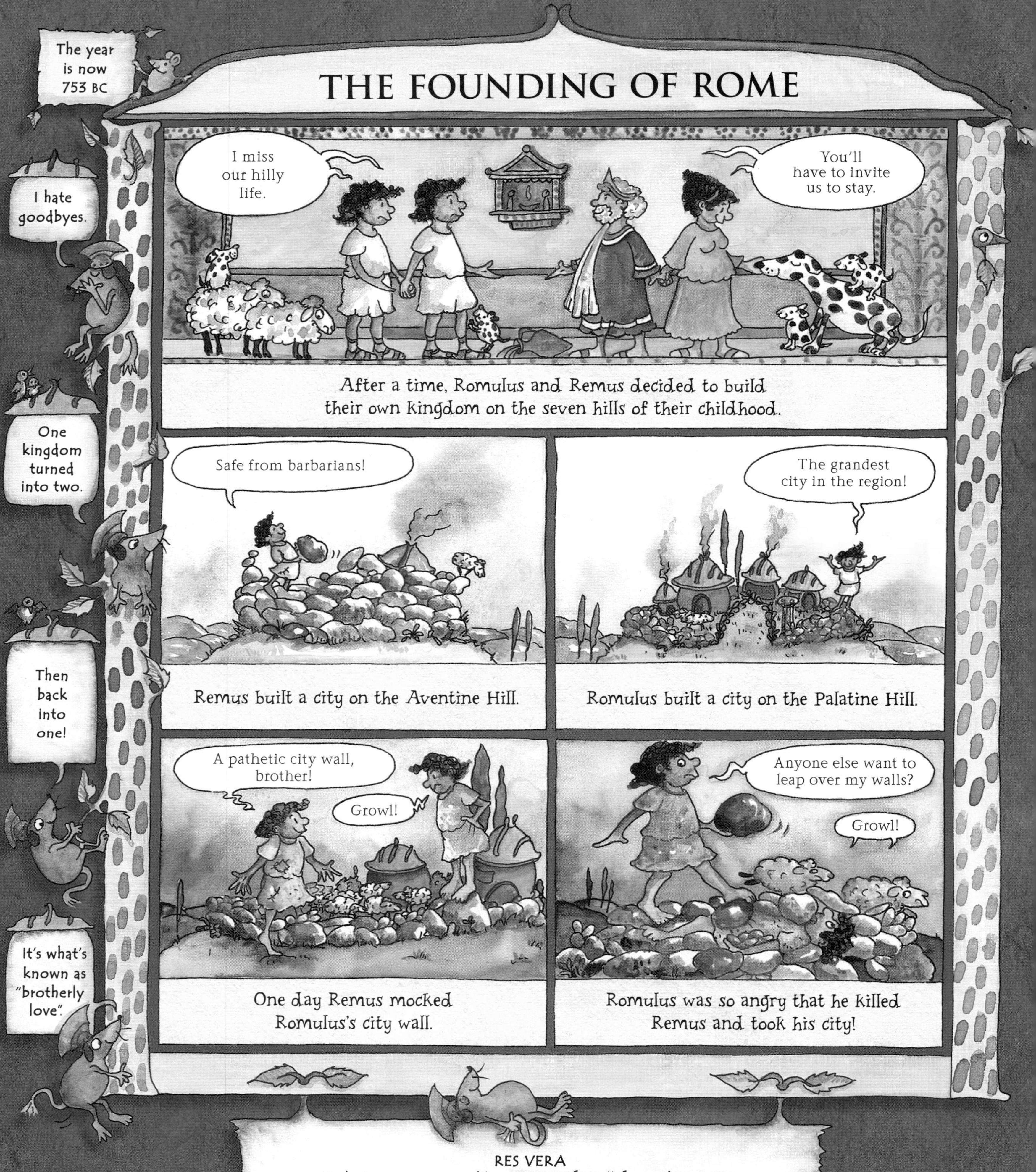
The year is now 753 BC
THE FOUNDING OF ROME
I hate goodbyes.
I miss our hilly life.
You'll have to invite us to stay.
After a time, Romulus and Remus decided to build their own kingdom on the seven hills of their childhood.
One kingdom turned into two.
Safe from barbarians!
Remus built a city on the Aventine Hill.
The grandest city in the region!
Romulus built a city on the Palatine Hill.
Then back into one!
A pathetic city wall, brother!
Growl!
One day Remus mocked Romulus's city wall.
Anyone else want to leap over my walls?
Growl!
Romulus was so angry that he killed Remus and took his city!
It's what's known as "brotherly love".

RES VERA

Early Rome was more like a group of small farms than a city.

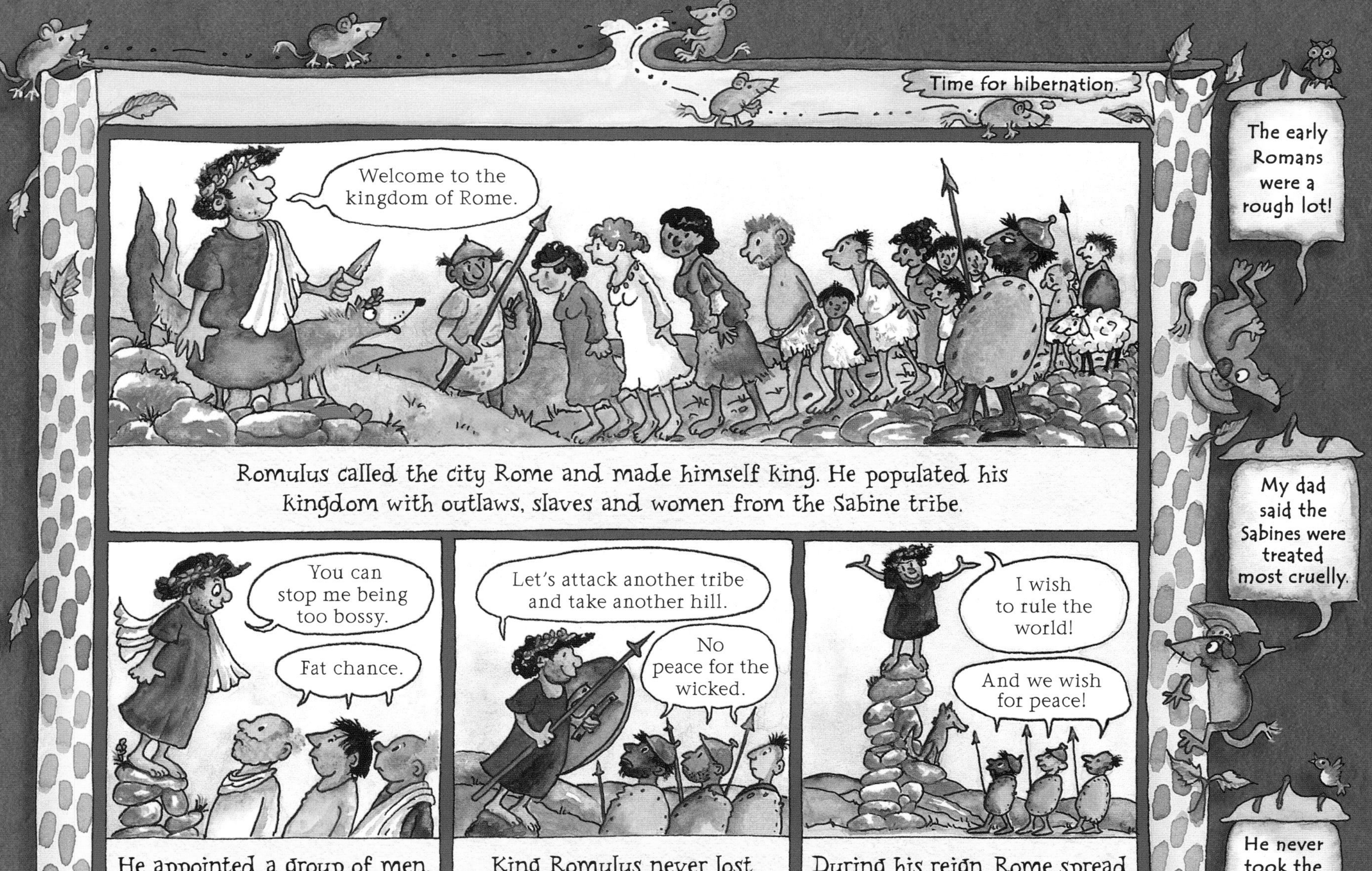

Time for hibernation.
Welcome to the kingdom of Rome.
Romulus called the city Rome and made himself king. He populated his kingdom with outlaws, slaves and women from the Sabine tribe.
The early Romans were a rough lot!
My dad said the Sabines were treated most cruelly.
You can stop me being too bossy.
Fat chance.
He appointed a group of men, called senators, to advise him.
Let's attack another tribe and take another hill.
No peace for the wicked.
King Romulus never lost his wild, war-like ways.
I wish to rule the world!
And we wish for peace!
During his reign, Rome spread across four of the seven hills.
He never took the advice of his senators.
We've lost the king!
Oh dear, oh dear.
He's totally vanished!
Then one day, in the midst of a thunderstorm, Mars spirited Romulus up to Mount Olympus and made him into a god named Quirinus.
I think Romulus got too bossy.

RES VERA

Many Romans believed Romulus hadn't really been spirited away to Mount Olympus but that he'd been assassinated by two senators who threw his body into the River Tiber.

THE SEVEN KINGS OF ROME

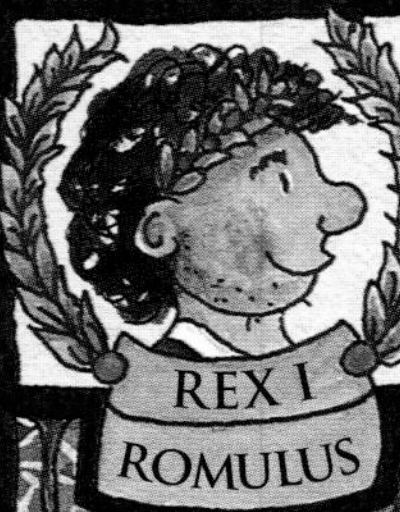
REX I
ROMULUS

Much of what we know about early Rome and its first seven kings comes from ancient stories. The Romans believed that Romulus and the six kings who followed him helped to create a structure for Roman society which lasted for hundreds of years.

Romulus exhausted the Romans with his battles.

Numa always listened to the gods – clever man!

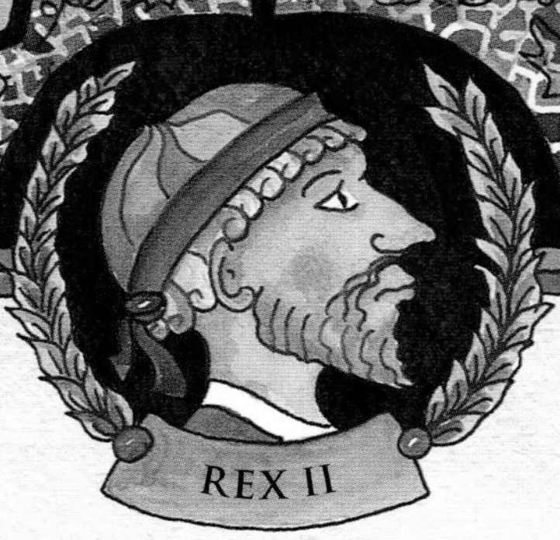
REX II

NUMA POMPILIUS 717–673 BC

After Romulus vanished, the Senate appointed a Sabine, Numa Pompilius, as Rome's new king. Numa was wise and peaceful, and he turned the wild barbarians of Romulus's reign into peaceful Roman citizens. They learned to respect other people's boundaries and to take pride in their crafts and trades. Numa died of old age.

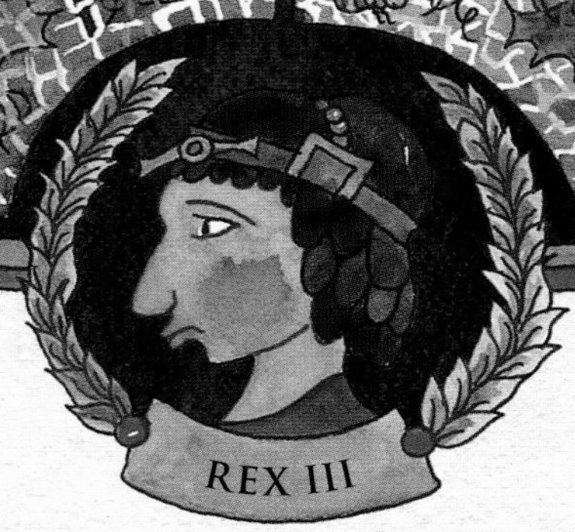
REX III

TULLIUS HOSTILIUS 673–642 BC

Tullius Hostilius was the third king of Rome. He never took advice from the gods and loved a good battle. He even destroyed Alba Longa, once ruled by King Numitor. When a terrible plague spread through Rome, Tullius became ill and turned to the gods for help. He was too late – Jupiter fired off a bolt of lightening, which hit Tullius's house and reduced it and Tullius to ashes!

The stories about these kings were written long after they'd died.

Not even a dormouse can tell what's true and what's false!

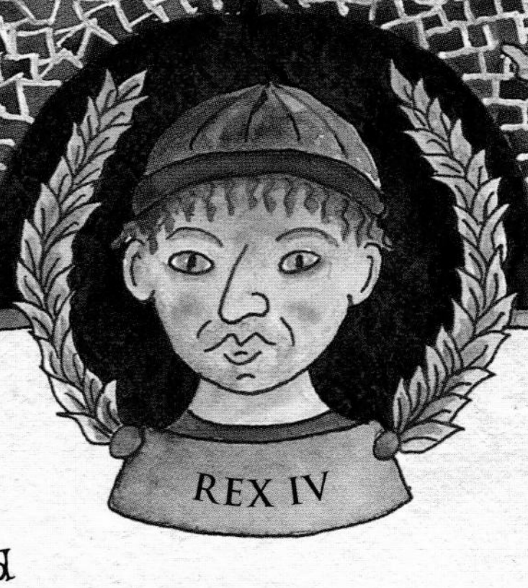
REX IV

ANCUS MARCIUS 642–616 BC

Ancus Marcius was the fourth king of Rome. He was the grandson of Numa Pompilius and he honoured the gods and wanted peace. King Ancus built the first bridge across the River Tiber and extended Rome's territory to the sea, founding the port of Ostia. He built a salt works there, which helped the Romans to preserve their food and make it tastier!

~~RES VERA~~ DORMOUSE FACT!

I, Dormeo, am the greatest Roman historian ever known to man or dormouse!

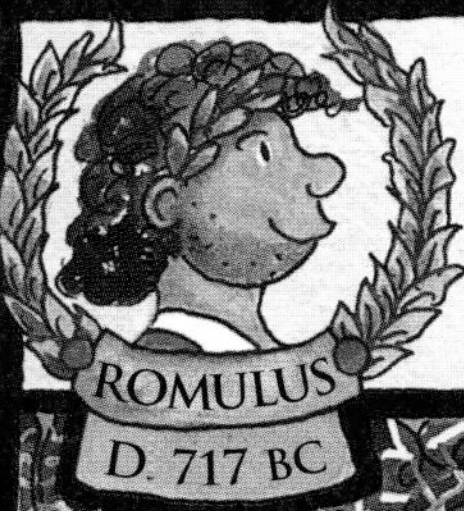
ROMULUS
D. 717 BC

The Rome that Romulus lived in was a collection of simple villages. As the population grew these were united into a city, and the Forum Romanum, Rome's first city centre, was built. As each king captured more land, Rome's influence spread.

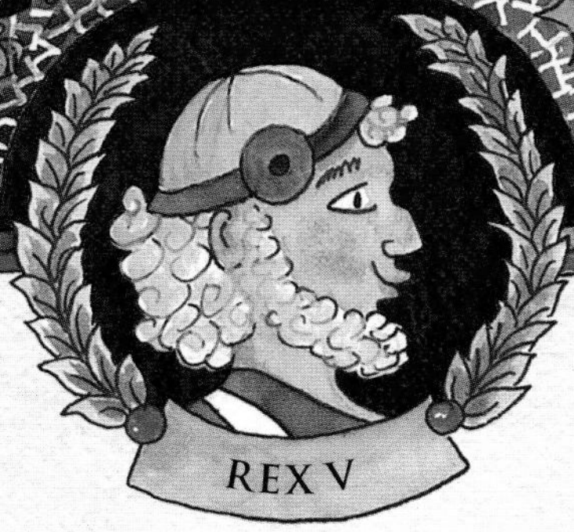
REX V

TARQUINIUS PRISCUS 616–579 BC

Tarquinius Priscus was the fifth king of Rome. He was the guardian of King Ancus's teenage sons and stole the throne from them. He built the first sewer, some great roads and the Circus Maximus for chariot racing and boxing. In the end, King Ancus's sons had him assassinated, but they still didn't get the throne as Tarquinius had already appointed his successor.

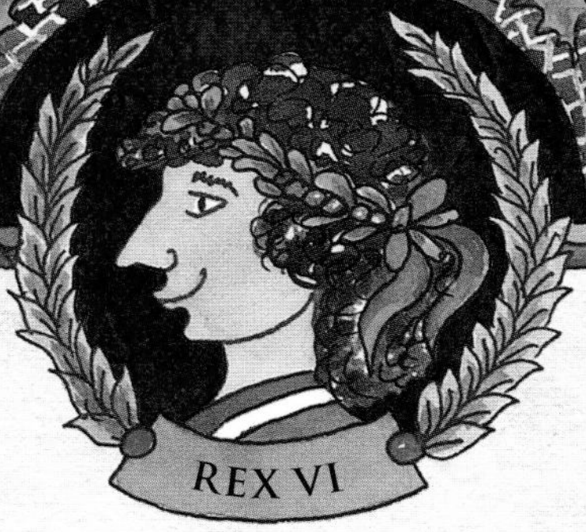
REX VI

SERVIUS TULLIUS 579–535 BC

Servius Tullius was the sixth king of Rome. He was born a slave, but was adopted by Tarquinius. He was caring and popular. Under his rule Rome grew to cover all seven hills, and the first Roman coins and census were introduced. Servius's reign ended when he was dragged from his throne and murdered by Tarquinius Priscus's grandson, Tarquinius Superbus.

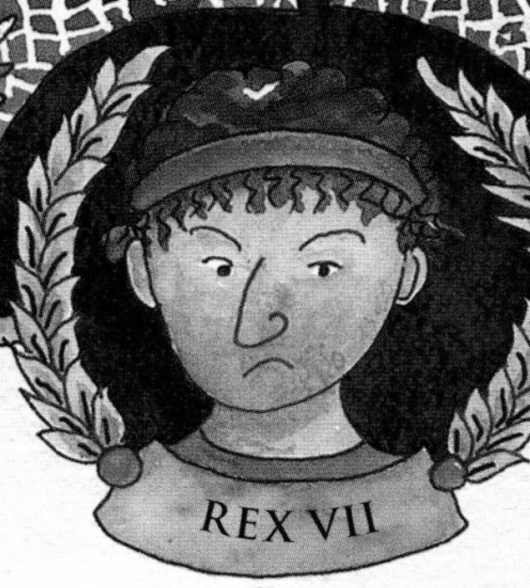
REX VII

TARQUINIUS SUPERBUS
535–509 BC

Tarquinius Superbus was the seventh and last king of Rome. The Roman people never forgave him for the murder of Servius Tullius. He ruled by fear and killed or persecuted anyone who disagreed with him and his son Sextus was no better. The pair behaved so abominably that the Roman people finally rebelled and drove Tarquinius into exile.

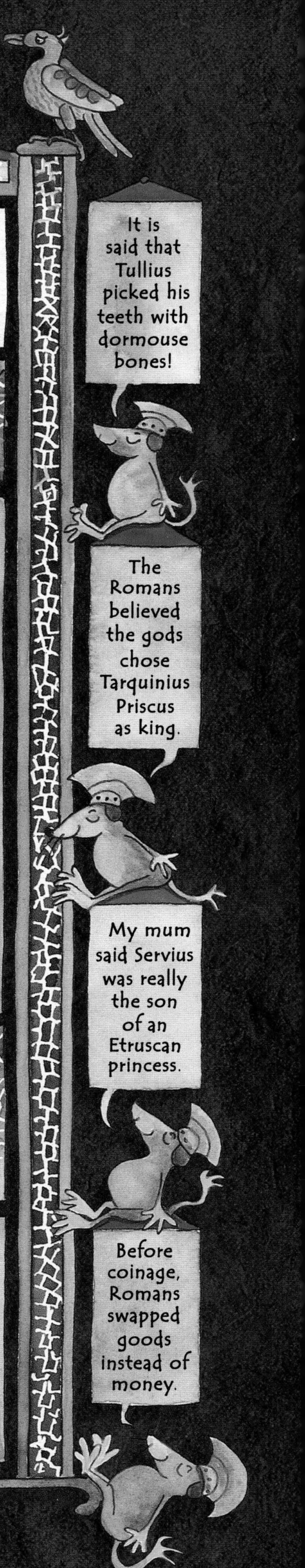
It is said that Tullius picked his teeth with dormouse bones!
The Romans believed the gods chose Tarquinius Priscus as king.
My mum said Servius was really the son of an Etruscan princess.
Before coinage, Romans swapped goods instead of money.

RES VERA

Servius Tullius organized the Romans into classes: patricians were landowners, equites were businessmen, plebeians were poor citizens, and slaves and people from outside Rome were non-citizens.

THE REPUBLIC OF ROME

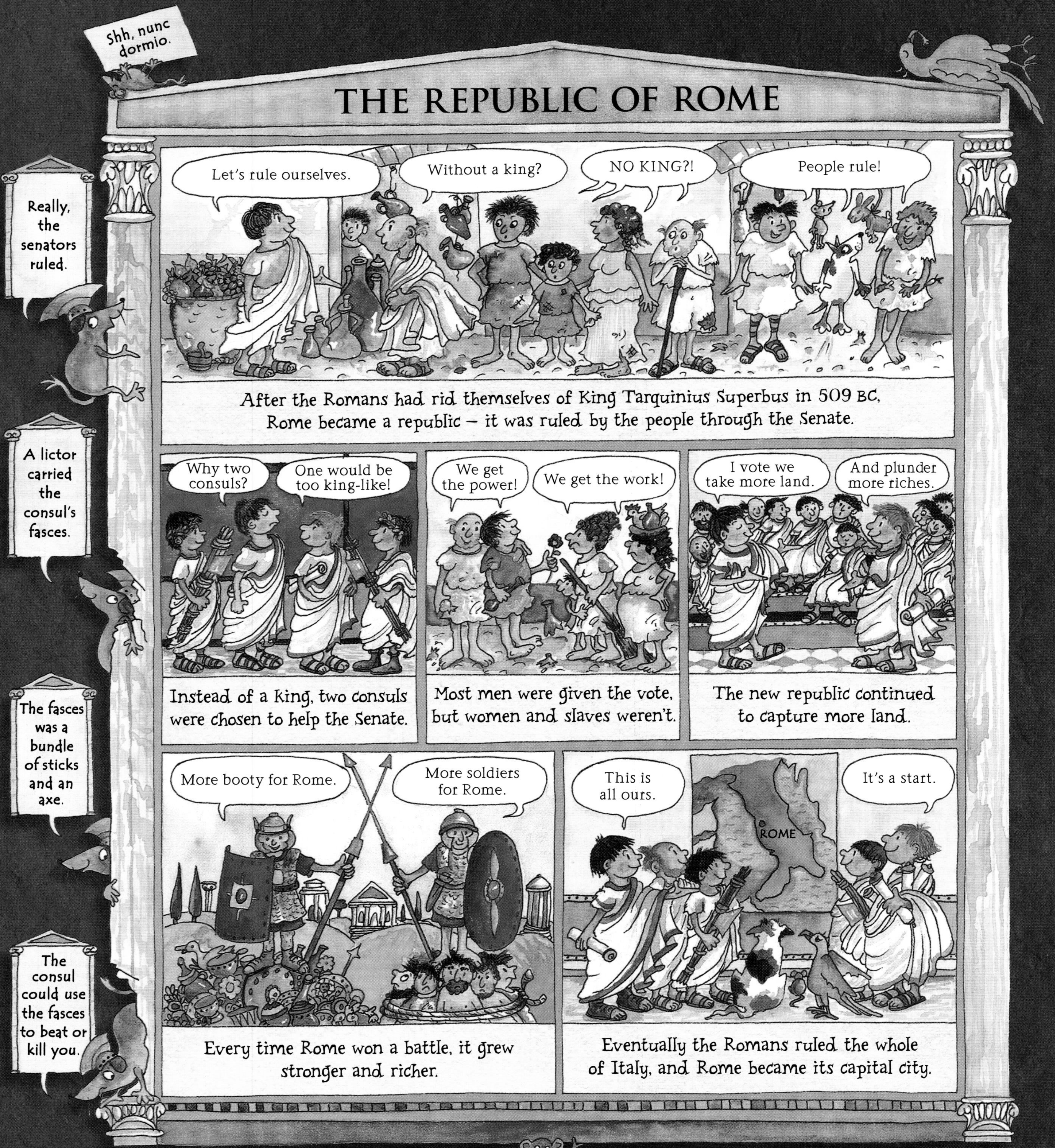
Shh, nunc dormio.
Let's rule ourselves.
Without a king?
NO KING?!
People rule!
After the Romans had rid themselves of King Tarquinius Superbus in 509 BC, Rome became a republic – it was ruled by the people through the Senate.
Really, the senators ruled.
Why two consuls?
One would be too king-like!
Instead of a King, two consuls were chosen to help the Senate.
We get the power!
We get the work!
Most men were given the vote, but women and slaves weren't.
I vote we take more land.
And plunder more riches.
The new republic continued to capture more land.
A lictor carried the consul's fasces.
The fasces was a bundle of sticks and an axe.
More booty for Rome.
More soldiers for Rome.
Every time Rome won a battle, it grew stronger and richer.
This is all ours.
ROME
It's a start.
Eventually the Romans ruled the whole of Italy, and Rome became its capital city.
The consul could use the fasces to beat or kill you.

RES VERA
A diet of dormice, grain and honey kept the Roman army fit.

THE GRUESOME GAULS

Shh, I'm still asleep.

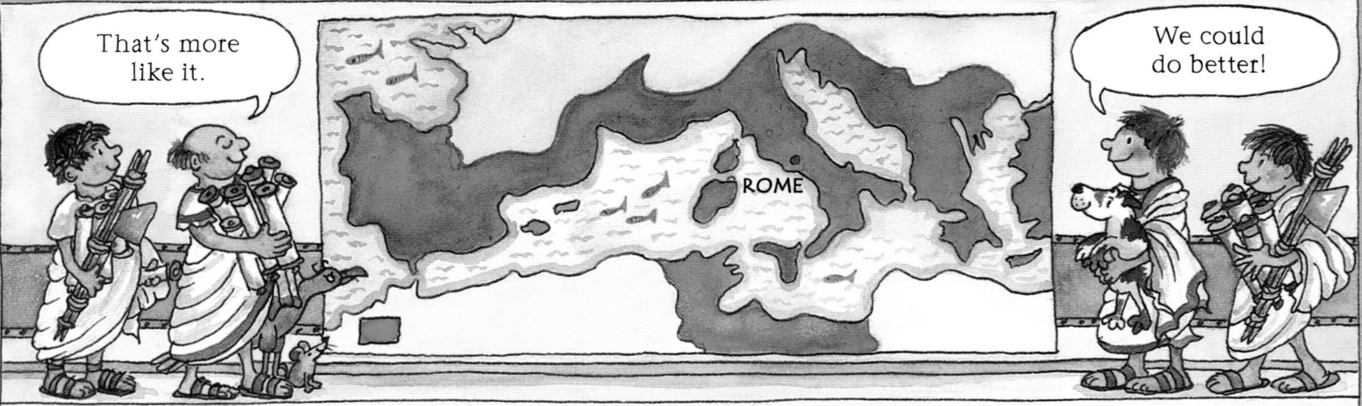
That's more like it.
ROME
We could do better!

The ambitious Romans fought on,
conquering lands around the Mediterranean Sea.

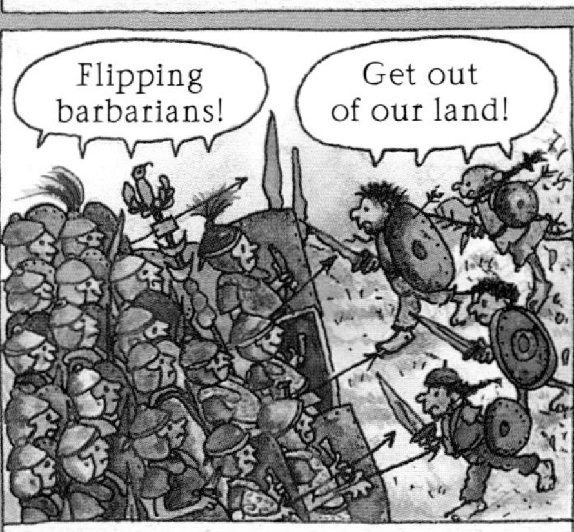
Flipping barbarians!
Get out of our land!

As Rome's power spread,
the barbarians fought back.

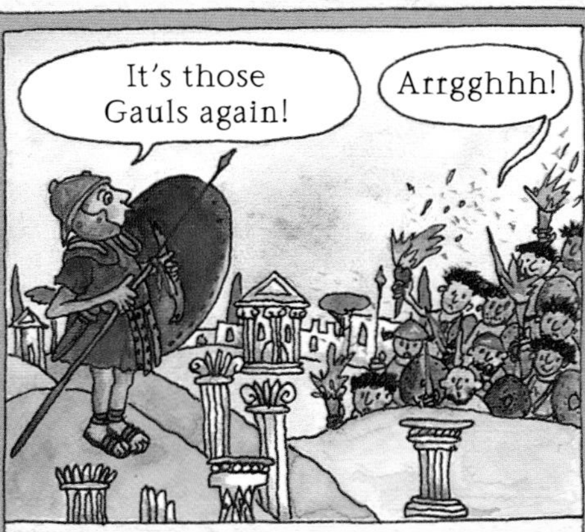
It's those Gauls again!
Arrgghhh!

In 390 BC, the Gauls from
Northern Europe invaded Rome.

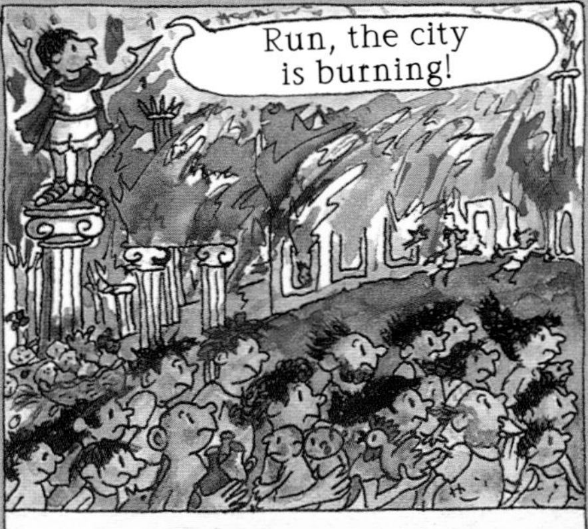
Run, the city is burning!

The Roman people fled
to the Capitol Hill.

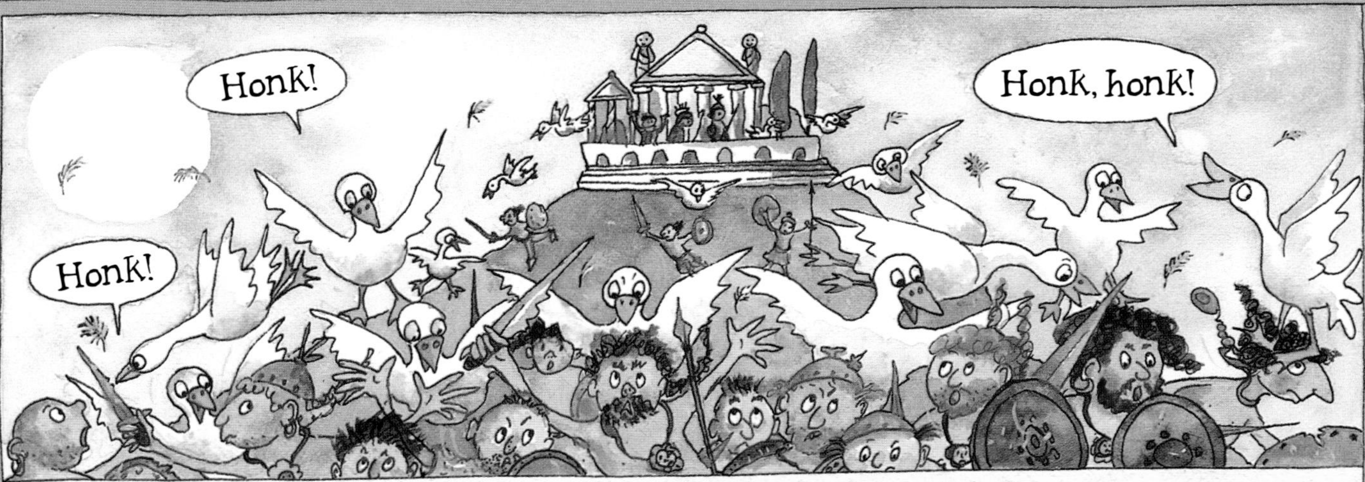
Honk!
Honk, honk!
Honk!

The Gauls attacked the Capitol under the cover of darkness.
The Romans were asleep, but luckily the sacred geese of Juno were keeping guard!
Their honking alerted the sleeping Romans and so saved the city.

Some fought for Rome, others for wealth and glory.

If you weren't a Roman, you were a barbarian!

The Gauls fought in the nude.

But they wore amulets to protect them!

Buzz, buzz!

~~RES VERA~~
DORMOUSE FACT!
I think it was the sight of the Gauls' naked bodies that started the geese honking!

JULIUS CAESAR

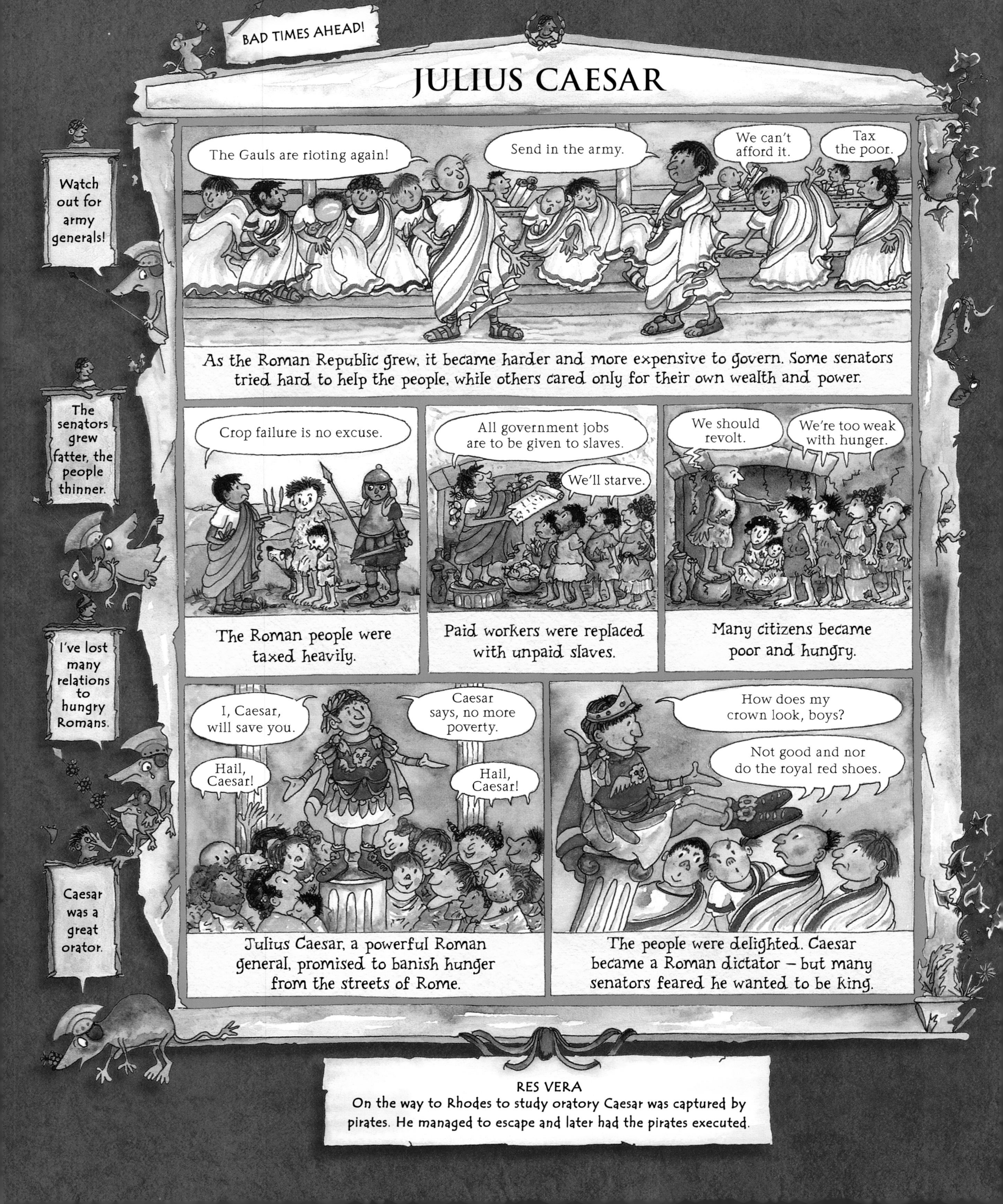
BAD TIMES AHEAD!
The Gauls are rioting again!
Send in the army.
We can't afford it.
Tax the poor.
As the Roman Republic grew, it became harder and more expensive to govern. Some senators tried hard to help the people, while others cared only for their own wealth and power.
Crop failure is no excuse.
The Roman people were taxed heavily.
All government jobs are to be given to slaves.
We'll starve.
Paid workers were replaced with unpaid slaves.
We should revolt.
We're too weak with hunger.
Many citizens became poor and hungry.
I, Caesar, will save you.
Caesar says, no more poverty.
Hail, Caesar!
Hail, Caesar!
Julius Caesar, a powerful Roman general, promised to banish hunger from the streets of Rome.
How does my crown look, boys?
Not good and nor do the royal red shoes.
The people were delighted. Caesar became a Roman dictator – but many senators feared he wanted to be king.
Watch out for army generals!
The senators grew fatter, the people thinner.
I've lost many relations to hungry Romans.
Caesar was a great orator.

RES VERA

On the way to Rhodes to study oratory Caesar was captured by pirates. He managed to escape and later had the pirates executed.

THE ROMAN EMPIRE

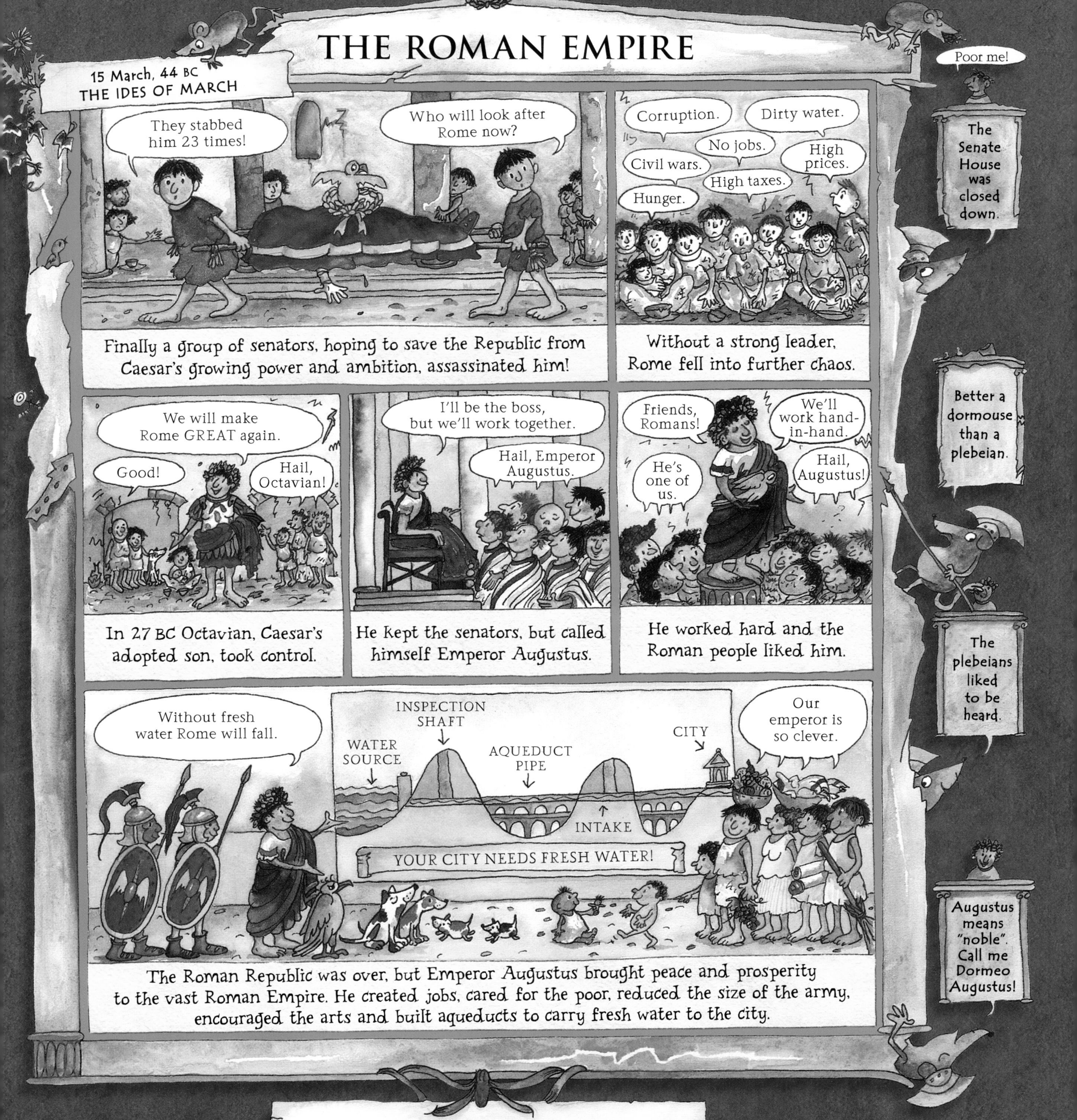

15 March, 44 BC
THE IDES OF MARCH
They stabbed him 23 times!
Who will look after Rome now?
Finally a group of senators, hoping to save the Republic from Caesar's growing power and ambition, assassinated him!
Corruption.
Dirty water.
No jobs.
Civil wars.
High prices.
High taxes.
Hunger.
Without a strong leader, Rome fell into further chaos.
Poor me!
The Senate House was closed down.
We will make Rome GREAT again.
Good!
Hail, Octavian!
In 27 BC Octavian, Caesar's adopted son, took control.
I'll be the boss, but we'll work together.
Hail, Emperor Augustus.
He kept the senators, but called himself Emperor Augustus.
Friends, Romans!
We'll work hand-in-hand.
He's one of us.
Hail, Augustus!
He worked hard and the Roman people liked him.
Better a dormouse than a plebeian.
The plebeians liked to be heard.
Without fresh water Rome will fall.
INSPECTION SHAFT
WATER SOURCE
AQUEDUCT PIPE
CITY
INTAKE
YOUR CITY NEEDS FRESH WATER!
Our emperor is so clever.
The Roman Republic was over, but Emperor Augustus brought peace and prosperity to the vast Roman Empire. He created jobs, cared for the poor, reduced the size of the army, encouraged the arts and built aqueducts to carry fresh water to the city.
Augustus means "noble". Call me Dormeo Augustus!

RES VERA
Caesar left his beautiful gardens by the River Tiber to the Roman people.

We lost our home to a Roman road!

CITIZENS OF THE EMPIRE

Emperor Augustus divided Rome into regions with wardens and appointed magistrates to care for the citizens. He also set up a night watch to guard against fire and had the River Tiber cleared of rubbish so that it stopped flooding the city.

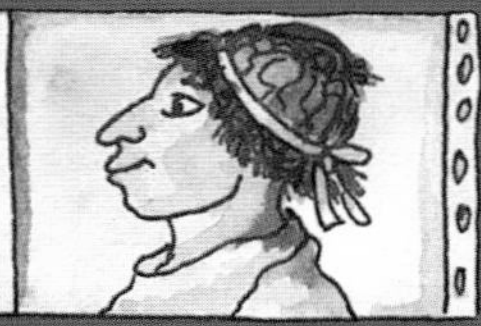

He should have cleared the cats out, too.

SENATORS

Senators came from wealthy families. Under Augustus they still issued laws, but these had to be approved by him.

Gladiatorial fights and chariot races also took place in the forum.

MAGISTRATES

This was another job for the wealthy. Magistrates were in charge of keeping law and order and collecting taxes.

A daily visit to the forum was a Roman must!

LANDOWNERS

A landowner might have an estate outside Rome which would be run by slaves who farmed food to be sold in the city.

Wait till you see my new helmet!

SOLDIERS

A young man from a wealthy family might join the army before going into politics. Legionaries had to sign up for 25 years!

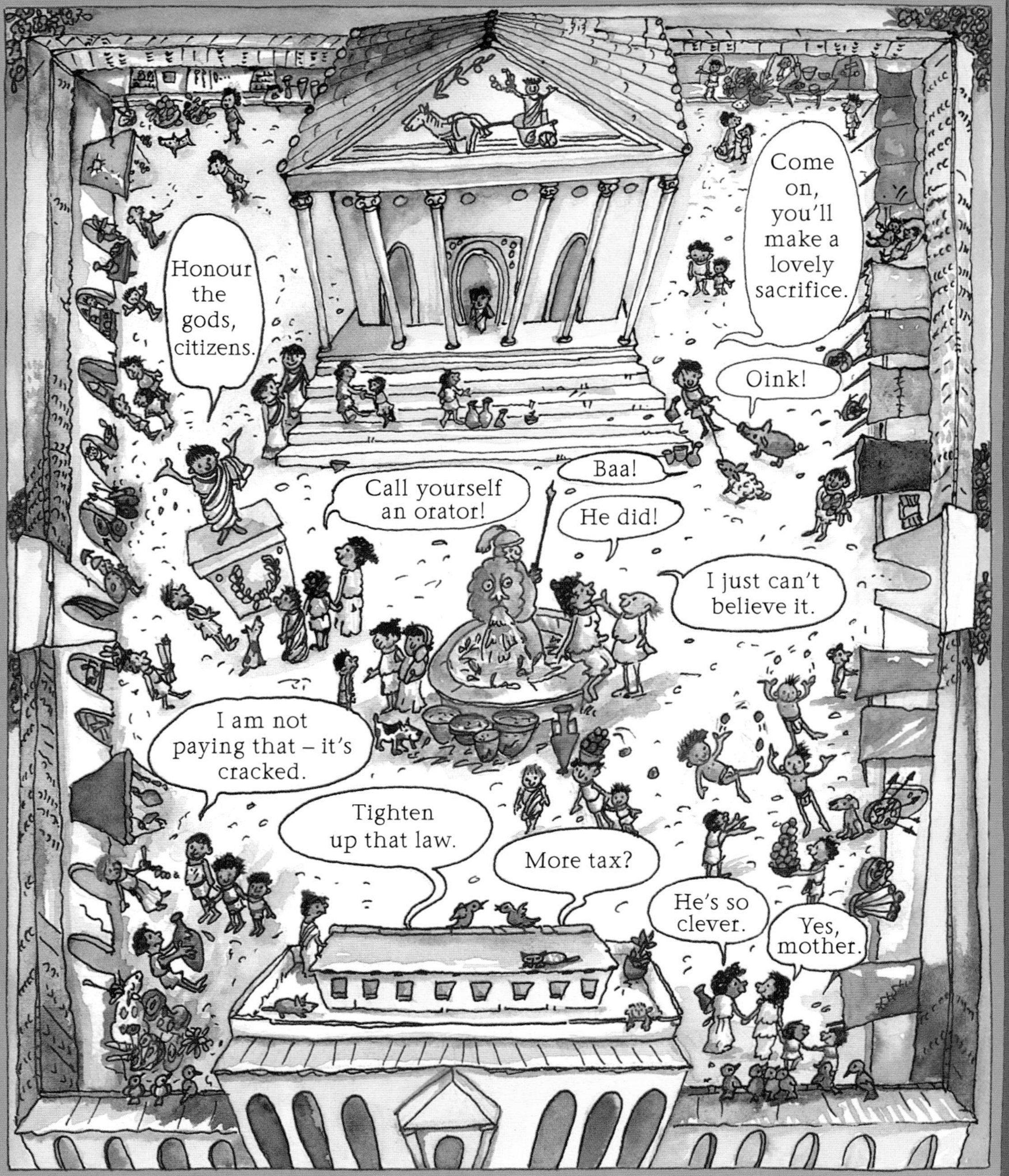

Honour the gods, citizens.
Come on, you'll make a lovely sacrifice.
Oink!
Baa!
Call yourself an orator!
He did!
I just can't believe it.
I am not paying that – it's cracked.
Tighten up that law.
More tax?
He's so clever.
Yes, mother.

THE FORUM was where everything happened – public speaking, banking, trading, trials, triumphal marches, festivals, shopping and gossiping! The Basilica, a public building, was at one end and a temple at the other.

RES VERA

Absolutely everyone, from powerful senators to poor slaves, met and mingled in the forum.

Only centurions or officers had crests on their helmet.

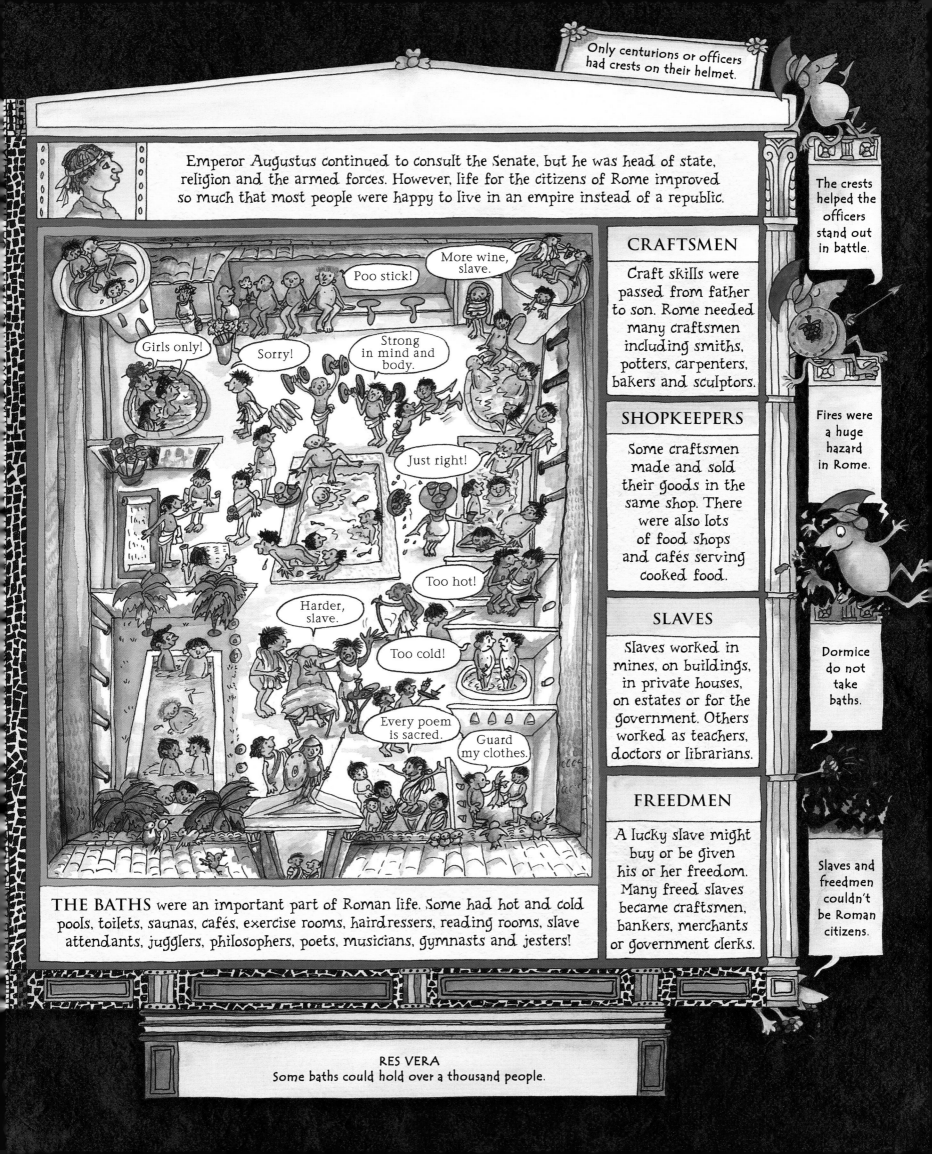

Emperor Augustus continued to consult the Senate, but he was head of state, religion and the armed forces. However, life for the citizens of Rome improved so much that most people were happy to live in an empire instead of a republic.

Poo stick!
More wine, slave.
Girls only!
Sorry!
Strong in mind and body.
Just right!
Too hot!
Harder, slave.
Too cold!
Every poem is sacred.
Guard my clothes.

THE BATHS were an important part of Roman life. Some had hot and cold pools, toilets, saunas, cafés, exercise rooms, hairdressers, reading rooms, slave attendants, jugglers, philosophers, poets, musicians, gymnasts and jesters!

CRAFTSMEN

Craft skills were passed from father to son. Rome needed many craftsmen including smiths, potters, carpenters, bakers and sculptors.

SHOPKEEPERS

Some craftsmen made and sold their goods in the same shop. There were also lots of food shops and cafés serving cooked food.

SLAVES

Slaves worked in mines, on buildings, in private houses, on estates or for the government. Others worked as teachers, doctors or librarians.

FREEDMEN

A lucky slave might buy or be given his or her freedom. Many freed slaves became craftsmen, bankers, merchants or government clerks.

The crests helped the officers stand out in battle.

Fires were a huge hazard in Rome.

Dormice do not take baths.

Slaves and freedmen couldn't be Roman citizens.

RES VERA
Some baths could hold over a thousand people.

My family are all nobiles.

PATRICIAN FAMILY LIFE

Family life was important to the Romans. The dad was head of the family. If he were rich (a patrician, or landowner), he would have a large house and many slaves. After breakfast, he might pray with his family at their shrine. Then he would walk to the forum to do a little trading, or visit the Senate.

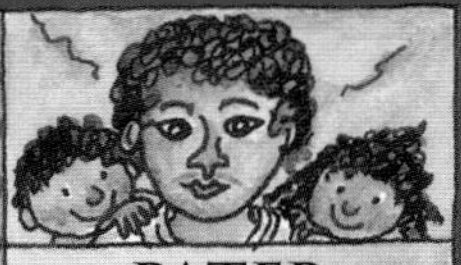

PATER

Many nobiles have a domus and a country villa.

All families honoured the gods.

They also consulted priests and fortune tellers.

Fortune tellers looked for signs in the weather and animal guts.

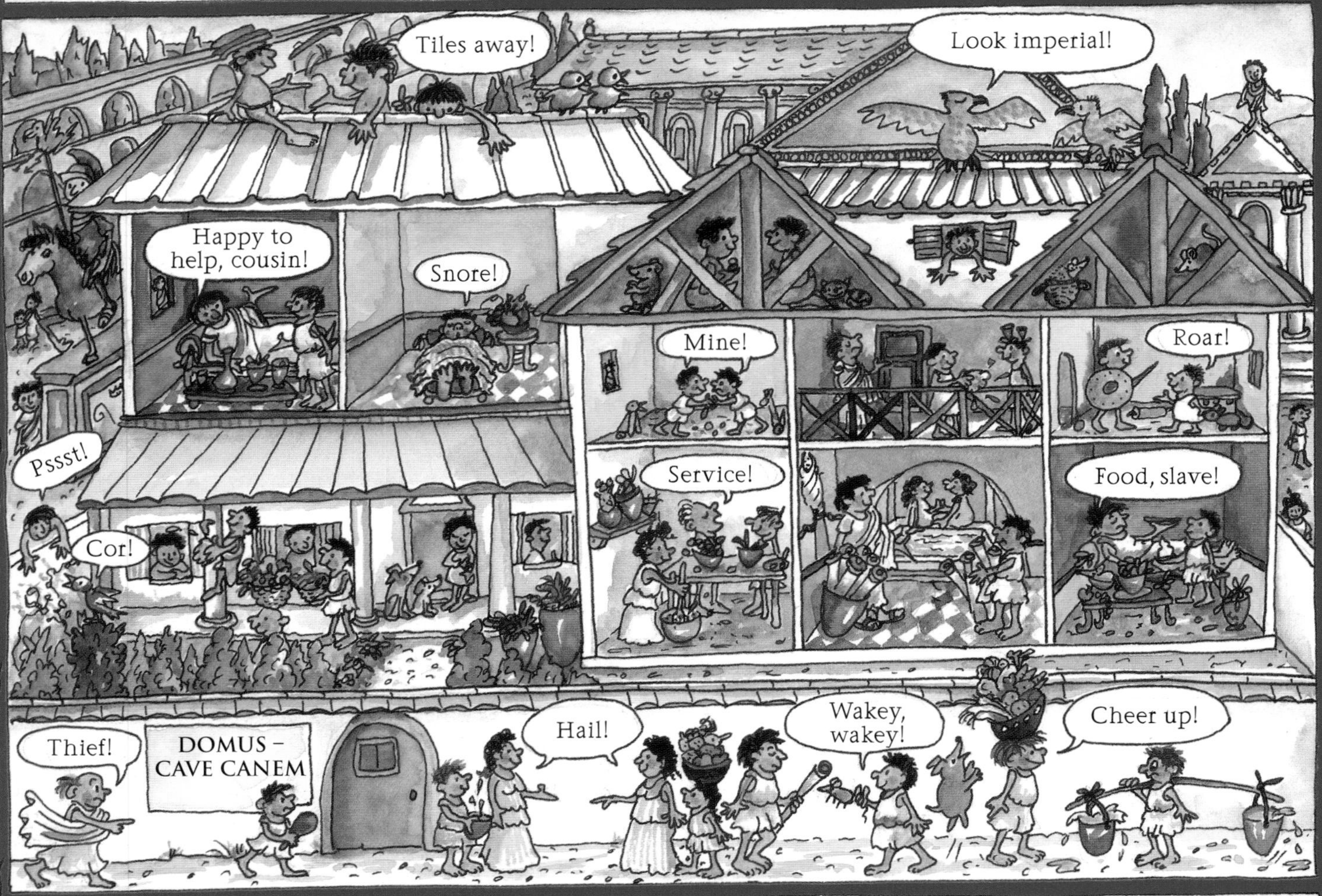
Tiles away!
Look imperial!
Happy to help, cousin!
Snore!
Mine!
Roar!
Pssst!
Service!
Food, slave!
Cor!
Thief!
DOMUS – CAVE CANEM
Hail!
Wakey, wakey!
Cheer up!

The patrician father would also meet with his poorer relations and former slaves, to see how they could be helped. After lunch, he might have a siesta followed by a visit to the baths. In the evening, friends might come for a dinner served by slaves, with other slaves playing music and dancing.

WOMEN

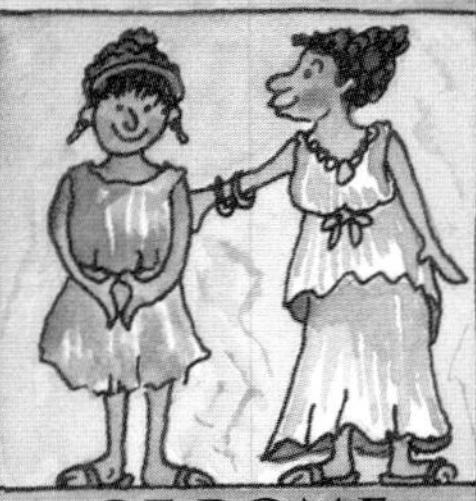

OF ROME

During the Republic, wealthy women did little but care for the household, but during the days of the Empire, many men were away fighting, which gave women more freedom. They still attended to their households, but encouraged by Emperor Augustus's powerful wife, Livia, they began to demand more independence and better education.

EMPRESS

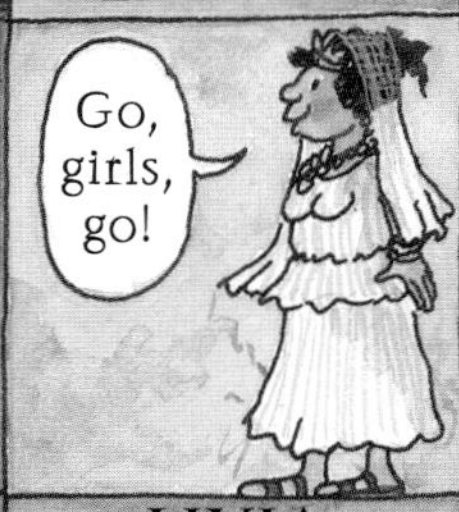
Go, girls, go!

LIVIA

RES VERA

The Roman Senate banned the eating of dormice in 115 BC – but that didn't stop people gobbling them up!

Dormice are NOT plebeians.

PLEBEIAN FAMILY LIFE

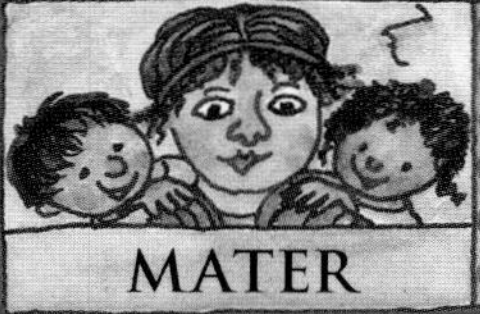
MATER

Even under Emperor Augustus, life was tough for the plebeians. If they weren't jobless and homeless, they lived in cramped rooms in high-rise flats. The top storeys were often built of wood, which was unsafe and a fire risk. During the summer, the heat was stifling and the streets stank of rotting rubbish and public toilets.

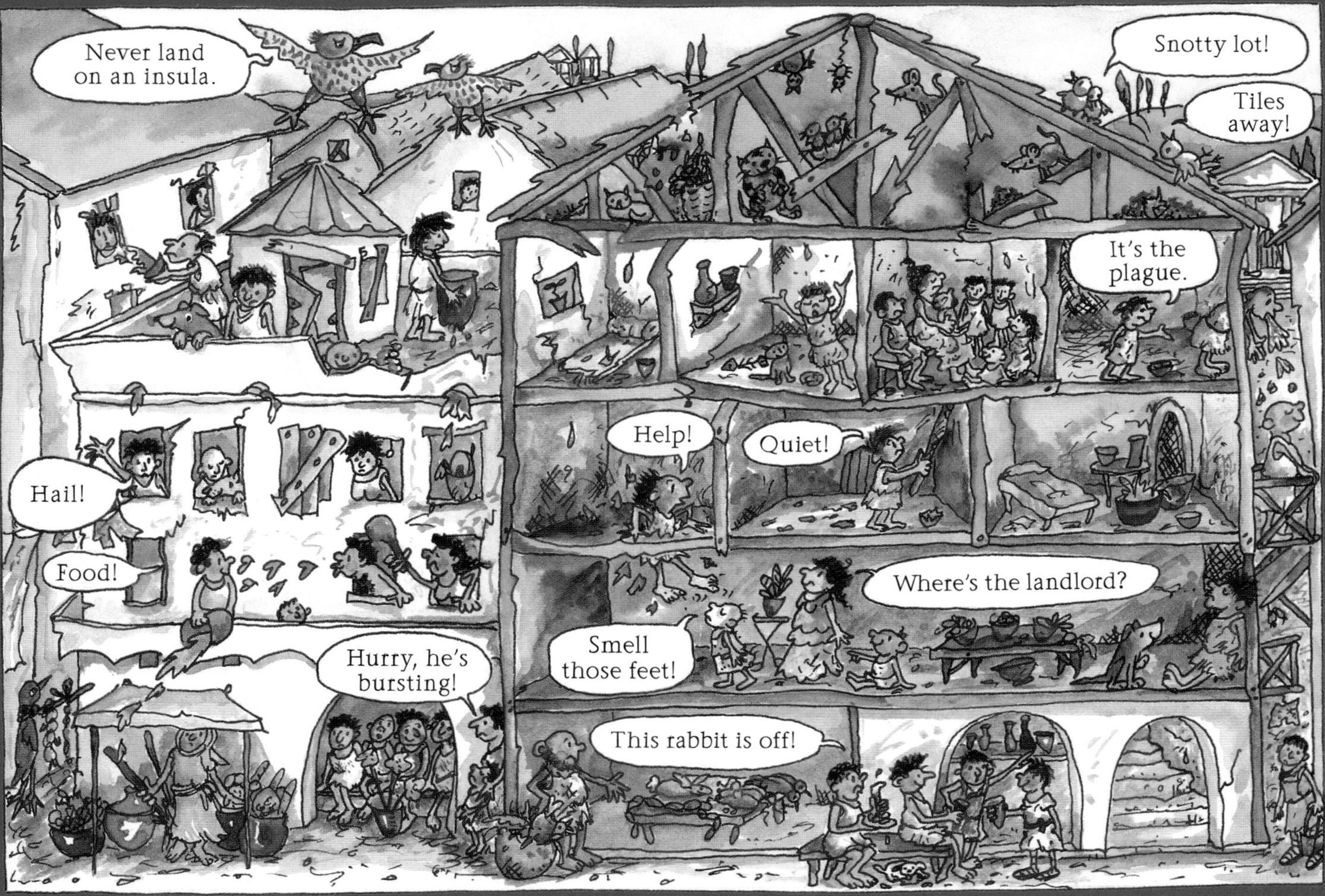
Never land on an insula.
Snotty lot!
Tiles away!
It's the plague.
Help!
Quiet!
Hail!
Food!
Where's the landlord?
Smell those feet!
Hurry, he's bursting!
This rabbit is off!

A plebeian would rise with the sun and go to bed when it got dark. Breakfast was likely to be a slice of bread and some olives. Then the whole family, including the youngest children, would go to work. As slaves did most of the manual work, plebeians worked as craftsmen, shopkeepers or on food stalls.

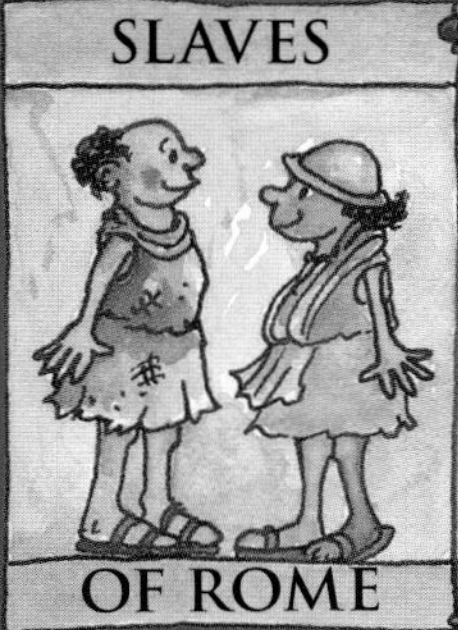
SLAVES
OF ROME

Some people were born into slavery while others were prisoners of war. There were slaves who were treated cruelly by their masters, but many others became trusted members of the household. If a slave child was lucky, he might even be adopted into the family.

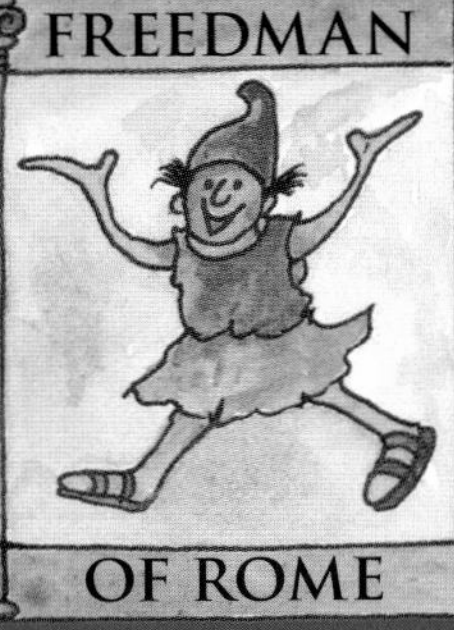
FREEDMAN
OF ROME

Plebeian families worked all day without rest.

Dormice sleep all day without rest!

Some plebeians joined the army.

Note the ex-slave's special freedman hat.

RES VERA
Roman houses could be crowded – sons lived with their parents even after they'd got married and had children!

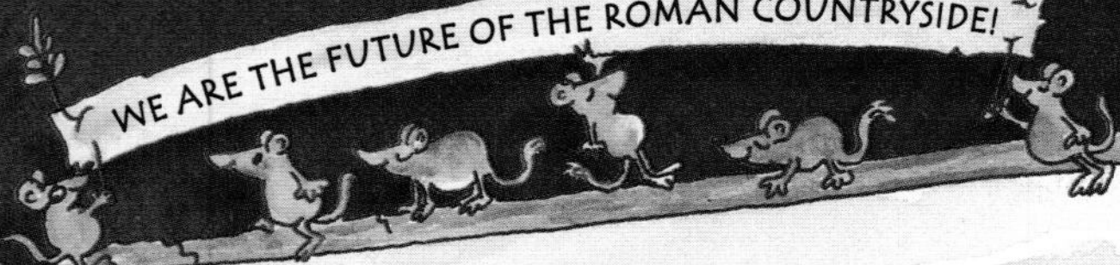
WE ARE THE FUTURE OF THE ROMAN COUNTRYSIDE!

THE CHILDREN OF ROME

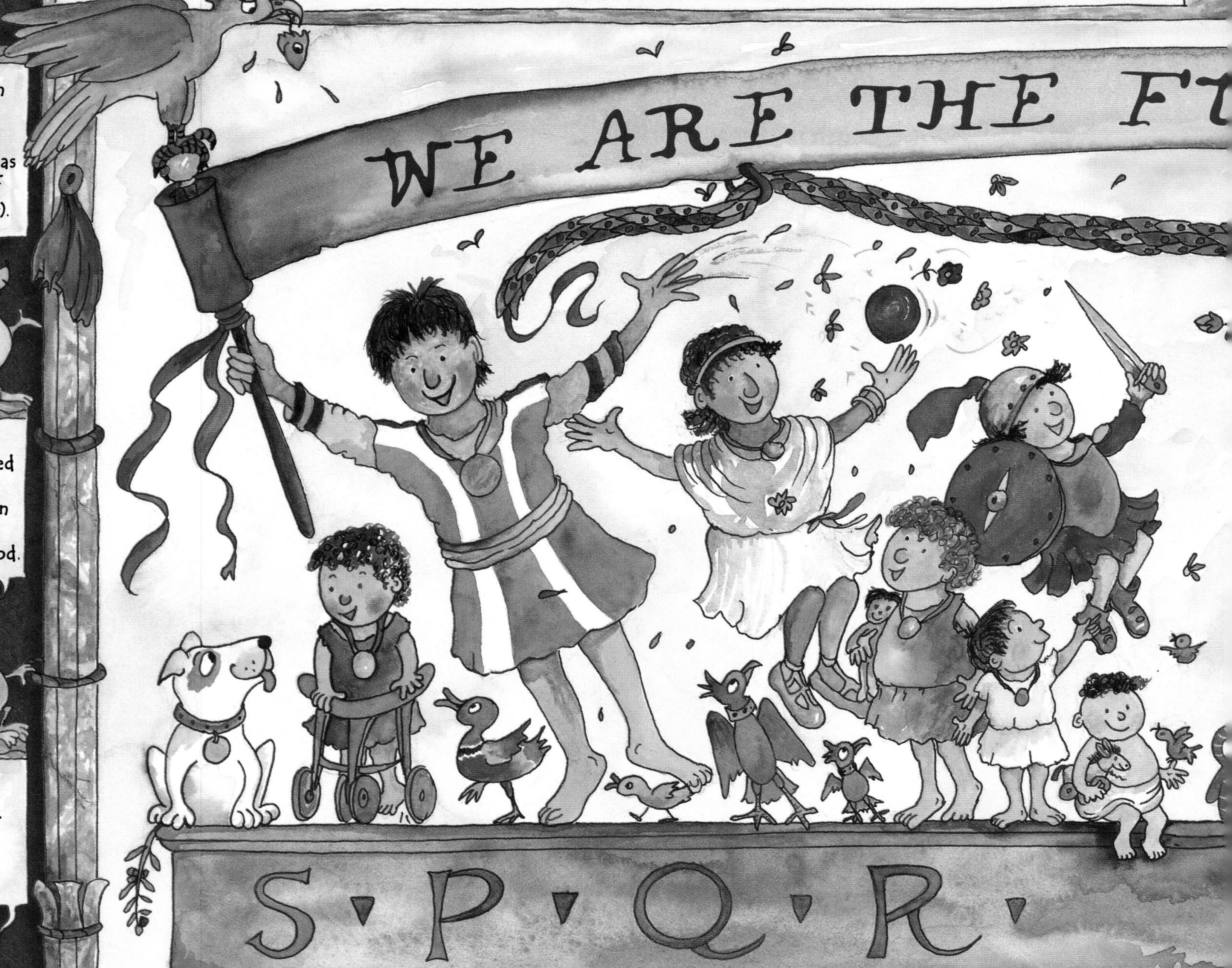
WE ARE THE FU
S · P · Q · R

A Roman father was the paterfamilias (head of the family).

He prepared his children for adulthood.

My father was eaten.

That's why Uncle Dormeo adopted me.

In the early days of ancient Rome, children had a tough time. Every baby was handed to its father and he would decide the newborn's fate. If the baby was weak, deformed or a second girl the father might decide not to keep it. The poor infant would be left to die or sold to a slave-trader.

RES VERA

Roman families often had lots of children as so many died either at birth or during early childhood.

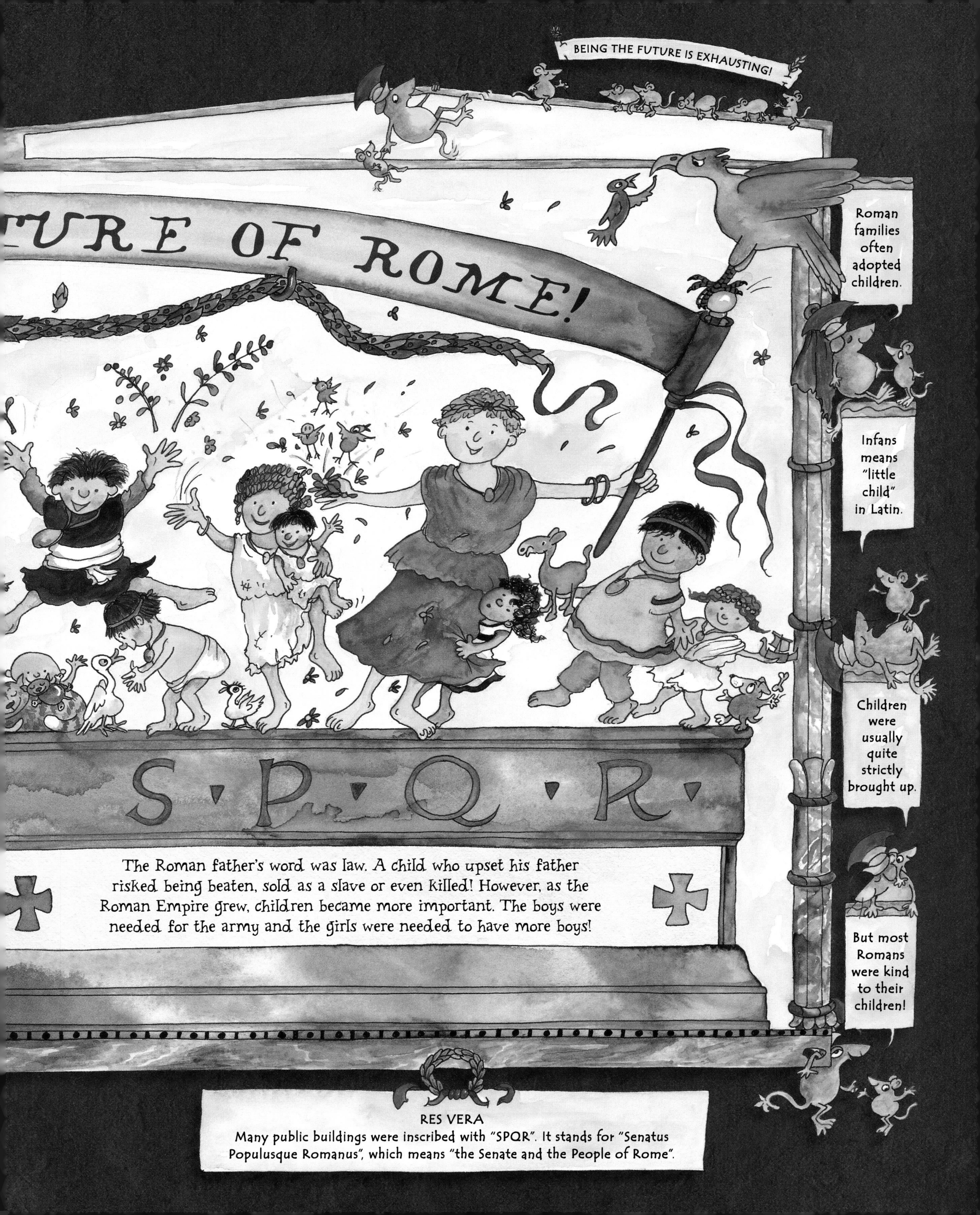
BEING THE FUTURE IS EXHAUSTING!
TURE OF ROME!
S · P · Q · R

Roman families often adopted children.

Infans means "little child" in Latin.

Children were usually quite strictly brought up.

But most Romans were kind to their children!

The Roman father's word was law. A child who upset his father risked being beaten, sold as a slave or even killed! However, as the Roman Empire grew, children became more important. The boys were needed for the army and the girls were needed to have more boys!

RES VERA

Many public buildings were inscribed with "SPQR". It stands for "Senatus Populusque Romanus", which means "the Senate and the People of Rome".

Most Romans were illiterate, unlike dormice.

A PATRICIAN CHILD'S DAY

PATRICIANS

Roman children born into a patrician family were very lucky. They were well fed, had nice homes and slaves to care for them. Their mother or father taught them their family duties and most children started school at the age of about six.

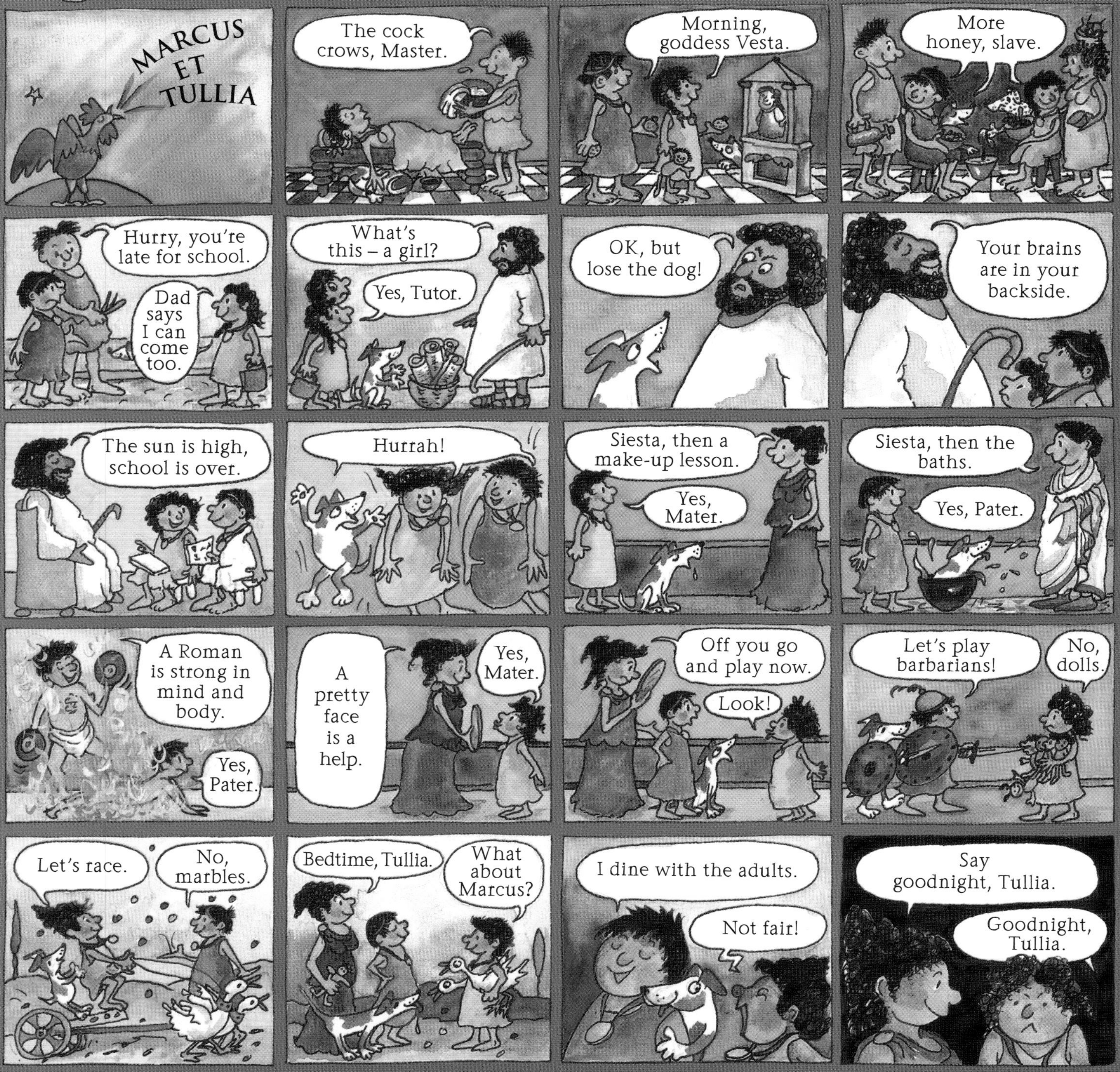

MARCUS ET TULLIA
The cock crows, Master.
Morning, goddess Vesta.
More honey, slave.
Hurry, you're late for school.
Dad says I can come too.
What's this – a girl?
Yes, Tutor.
OK, but lose the dog!
Your brains are in your backside.
The sun is high, school is over.
Hurrah!
Siesta, then a make-up lesson.
Yes, Mater.
Siesta, then the baths.
Yes, Pater.
A Roman is strong in mind and body.
Yes, Pater.
A pretty face is a help.
Yes, Mater.
Off you go and play now.
Look!
Let's play barbarians!
No, dolls.
Let's race.
No, marbles.
Bedtime, Tullia.
What about Marcus?
I dine with the adults.
Not fair!
Say goodnight, Tullia.
Goodnight, Tullia.

A ludus was a primary school.

At eleven, you moved to the grammaticus.

As you can tell, I went to both.

We both ate our wax tablets!

RES VERA
At the ludus pupils studied in Latin, and at the grammaticus they studied in Greek.

Rome was always noisy.

A PLEBEIAN CHILD'S DAY

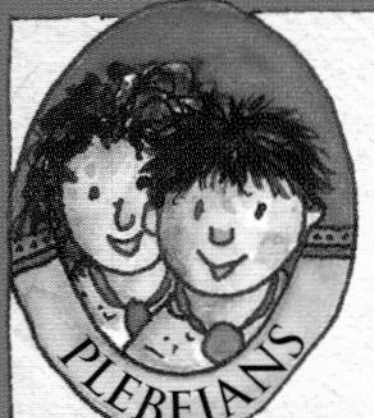
PLEBEIANS

Plebeian children had a much rougher time and very short childhoods. They often had poor diets and cramped, unhygienic homes, so many died of infection or disease. Few plebeian children went to school because they had to start work at the age of five or six.

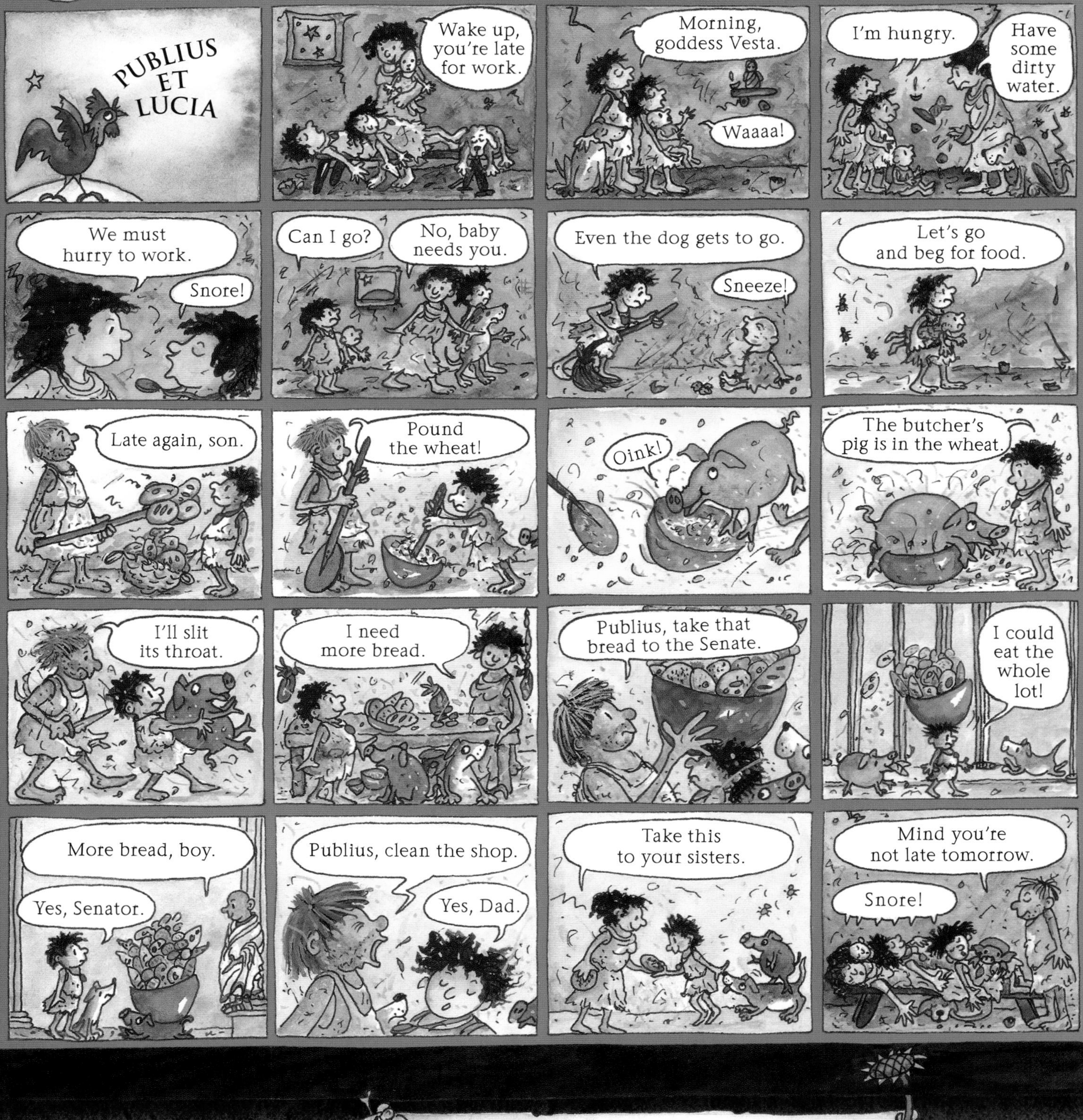
PUBLIUS ET LUCIA
Wake up, you're late for work.
Morning, goddess Vesta.
Waaaa!
I'm hungry.
Have some dirty water.
We must hurry to work.
Snore!
Can I go?
No, baby needs you.
Even the dog gets to go.
Sneeze!
Let's go and beg for food.
Late again, son.
Pound the wheat!
Oink!
The butcher's pig is in the wheat.
I'll slit its throat.
I need more bread.
Publius, take that bread to the Senate.
I could eat the whole lot!
More bread, boy.
Yes, Senator.
Publius, clean the shop.
Yes, Dad.
Take this to your sisters.
Mind you're not late tomorrow.
Snore!

Wheeled traffic could only enter Rome at night.

All goods rumbled into the city after dark.

By day, beggars lined the roads.

Every nine days there was a slave market.

RES VERA
If plebeian children were not out at work by the age of six, they were probably looking after their siblings.

FESTIVALS

January: Parentalia Festival, for dead parents

March: the feast of Mars

April: the founding of Rome

August: the feast of Mercury

The ancient Romans loved to celebrate. They had over 200 festivals a year, celebrating everything from the gods to their own greatness! The nobles would pay for plays, pantomimes, dancing, games or feasts, which often lasted several days.
On 1 March, buildings were hung with laurels to celebrate the Roman New Year.

RES VERA
On 17 December, the feast of Saturnalia started. Pigs were sacrificed then served to slaves by their masters.

GLADIATORS

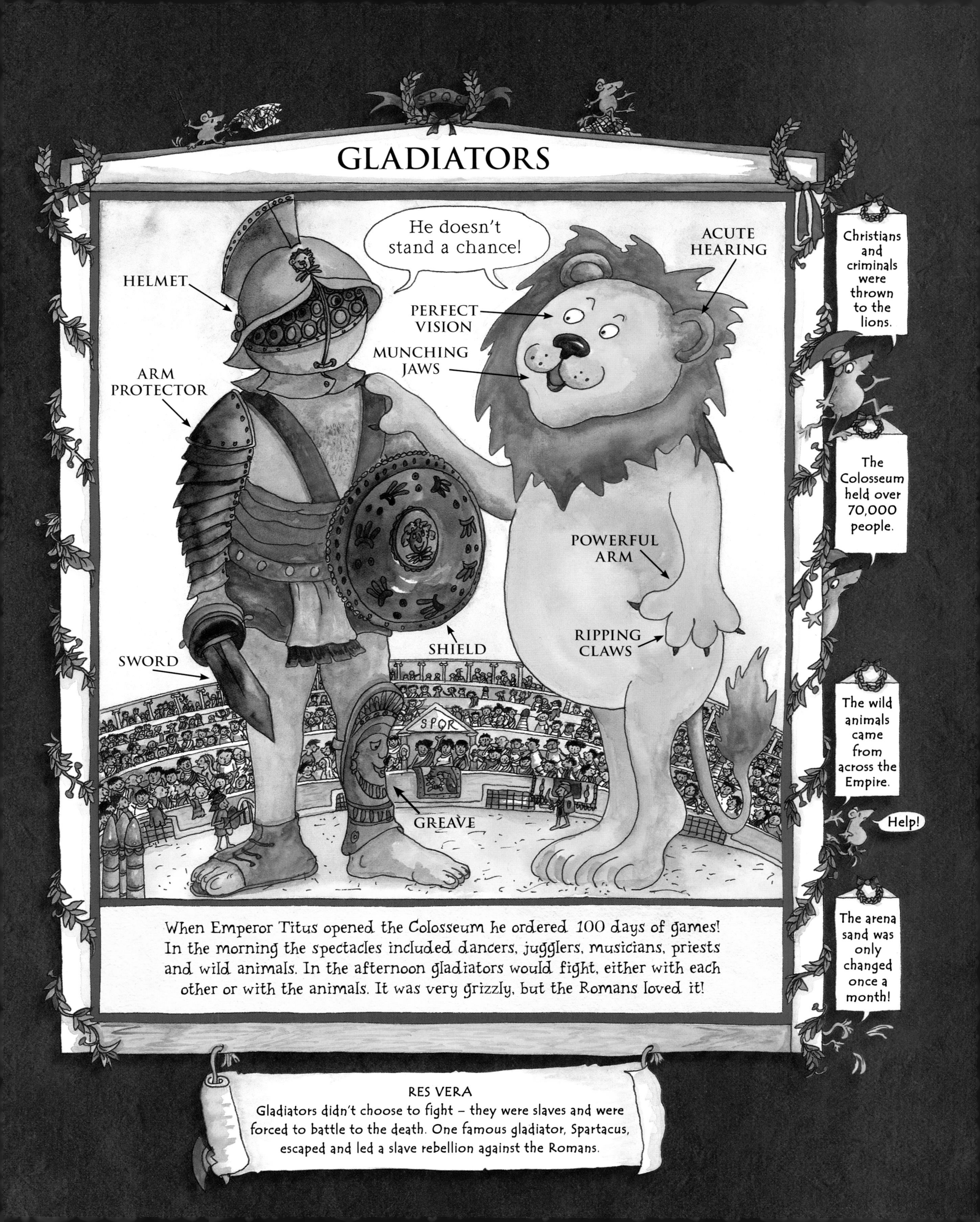

He doesn't stand a chance!
HELMET
ARM PROTECTOR
SWORD
SHIELD
GREAVE
PERFECT VISION
MUNCHING JAWS
ACUTE HEARING
POWERFUL ARM
RIPPING CLAWS
SPQR
Help!

When Emperor Titus opened the Colosseum he ordered 100 days of games! In the morning the spectacles included dancers, jugglers, musicians, priests and wild animals. In the afternoon gladiators would fight, either with each other or with the animals. It was very grizzly, but the Romans loved it!

Christians and criminals were thrown to the lions.

The Colosseum held over 70,000 people.

The wild animals came from across the Empire.

The arena sand was only changed once a month!

RES VERA

Gladiators didn't choose to fight – they were slaves and were forced to battle to the death. One famous gladiator, Spartacus, escaped and led a slave rebellion against the Romans.

THE GREAT ROMAN ARMY

Centurions used a vine cane for beating their legionaries.

Legionaries bribed centurions to avoid a duty or punishment.

Legionaries were given financial rewards for victories.

Coronae, military crowns, were awarded for bravery.

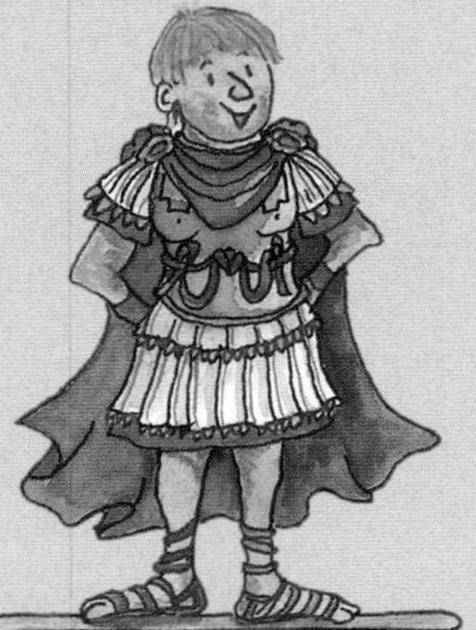

LEGATUS

The legion commander and camp prefect, the legatus was usually a senator appointed by the emperor.

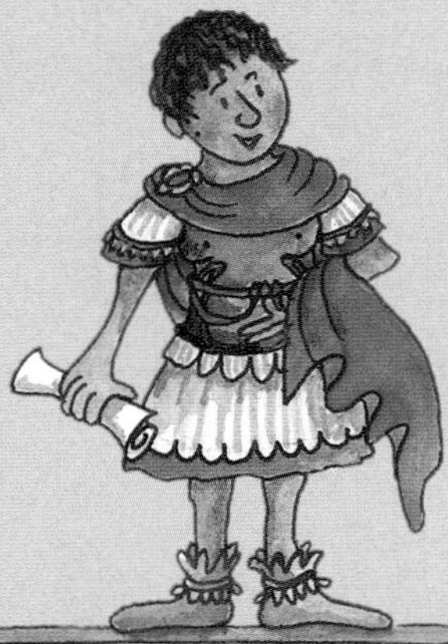

TRIBUNE

There were six tribunes in each legion. The chief tribune was a young noble waiting to join the Senate.

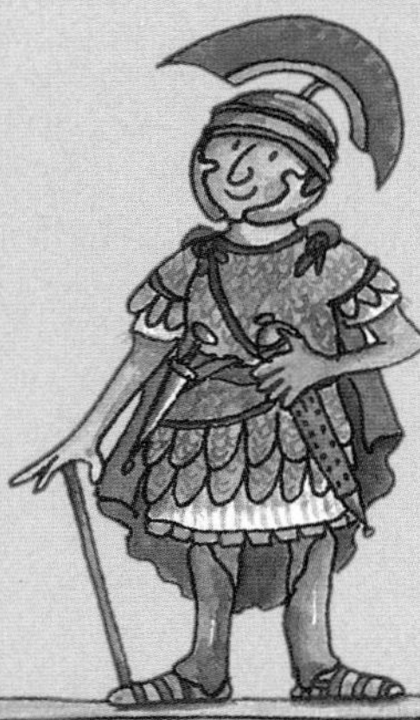

CENTURION

There were 59 centurions in command of each legion. They usually rose from the ranks.

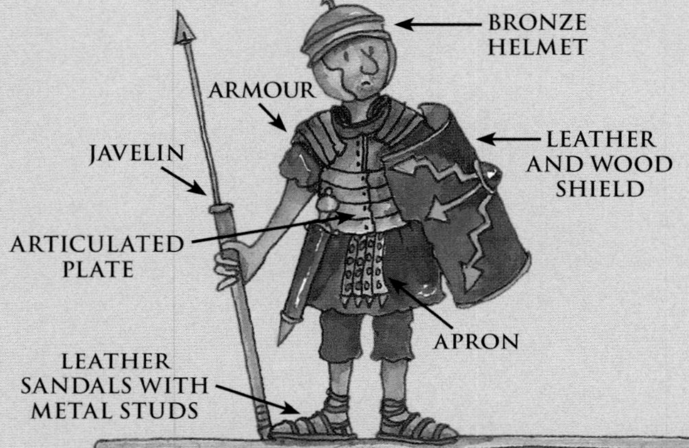
BRONZE HELMET
ARMOUR
JAVELIN
LEATHER AND WOOD SHIELD
ARTICULATED PLATE
APRON
LEATHER SANDALS WITH METAL STUDS

LEGIONARY

Training was tough for legionaries. They learned to march, swim, build camps, vault horses and use a variety of weapons.

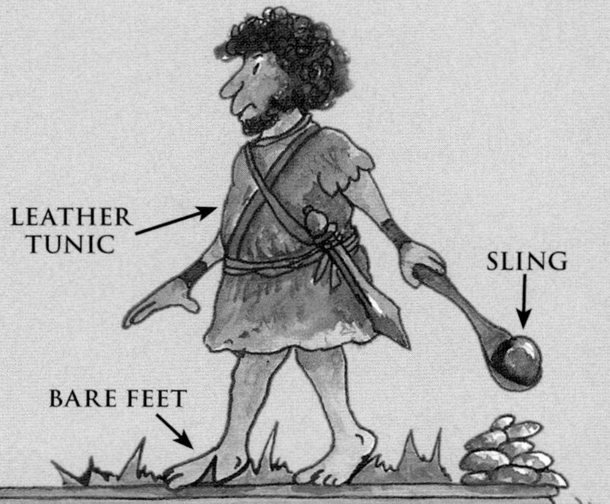
LEATHER TUNIC
SLING
BARE FEET

AUXILIARY

Auxiliaries were support soldiers. They earned less and had less training than legionaries.

Without the amazing and totally brilliant Roman army, Rome might never have ruled such a vast empire. In the early days soldiers were part-time, but as the Empire grew a full-time army was needed. By AD 200, the Roman army had about 300,000 career soldiers. They were skilled, well-disciplined, fit and determined! As well as learning to fight, some soldiers were trained as surveyors, engineers and stonemasons. They supervized the construction of canals, bridges and a vast network of roads.

RES VERA

The most prized military crown was the corona graminea, presented to a commander who had saved the whole legion or the entire army.

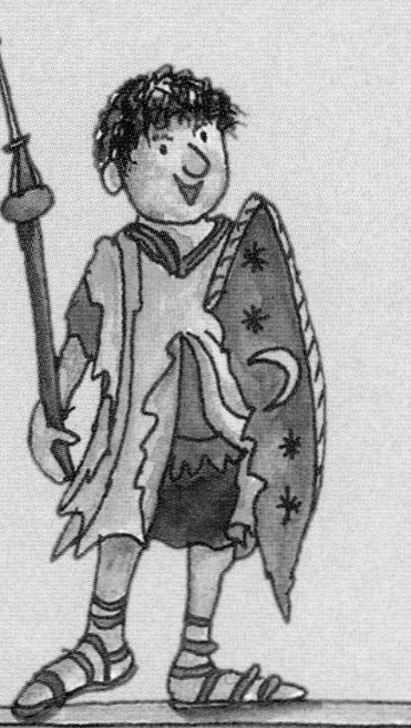

PRAETORIAN GUARD

These were the emperor's personal bodyguards. New emperors gave them huge bonuses to make them loyal. It didn't always work!

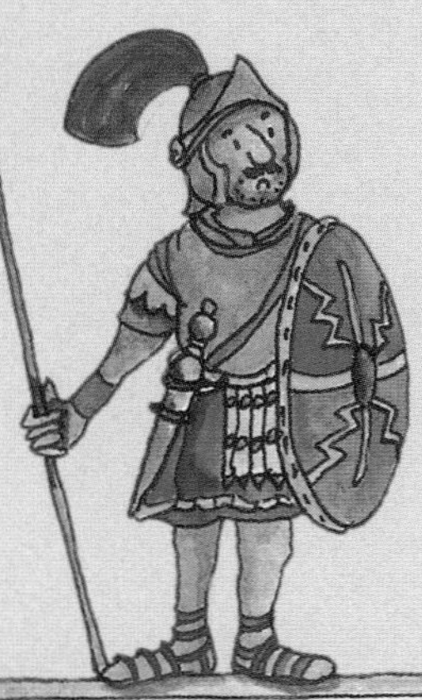

URBAN COHORTS

The urban cohorts acted as the police force in Rome. They were under the command of the city prefect.

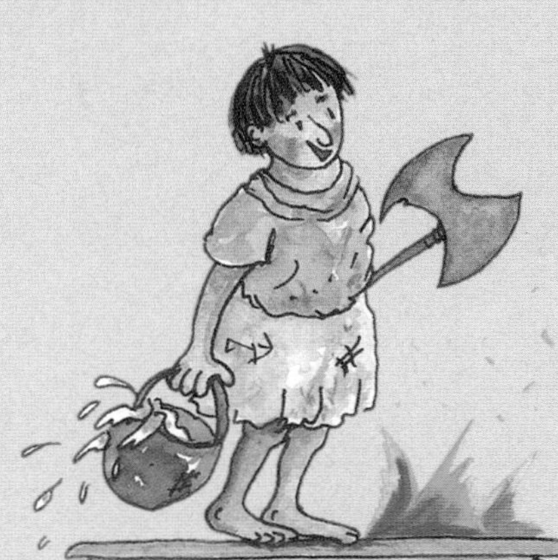

VIGILES

A semi-military force which acted as the fire service and the night police for the fourteen districts of Rome.

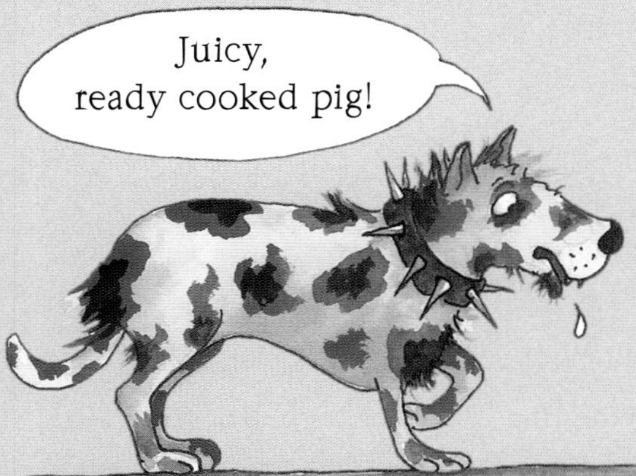
Juicy, ready cooked pig!

WAR DOG

Attack formations were sometimes made up entirely of well-trained, hungry dogs.

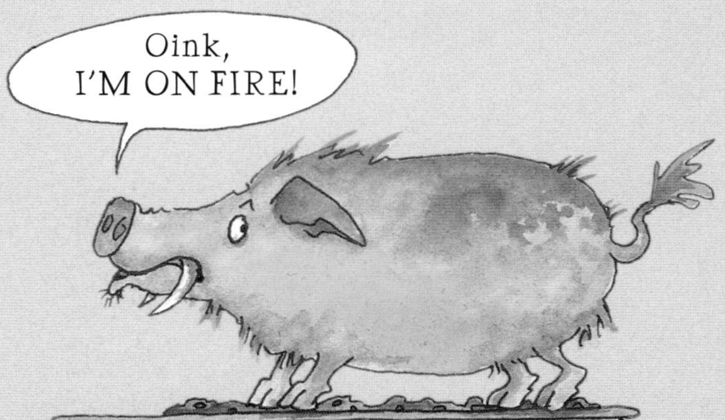
Oink, I'M ON FIRE!

WAR PIG

Pigs were covered in resin and set on fire. Their squealing terrified enemy elephants!

The main strength of the army were the legionaries, recruited from Roman citizens. There were about 5,000 men in a legion, divided into centuries of 80 men. Each legion also had about 5,000 auxiliaries, who were non-citizens. They served as border guards or specialist soldiers like archers and cavalrymen. The army was a good career for poor men … if they survived the 25 years they had to sign up for! On retirement a citizen was given a small pension and plot of land, while a non-citizen was given Roman citizenship.

Rome had three urban cohorts of 1,000 men each.

In early Rome there were no prisons for criminals.

Criminals were fined, exiled or lost their citizenship.

Dormice were sometimes eaten with a pig meat stuffing!

RES VERA

Many people think that a vomitorium was a room where Romans made themselves sick after eating too much – but it was actually the name for a passageway at the back of an amphitheatre!

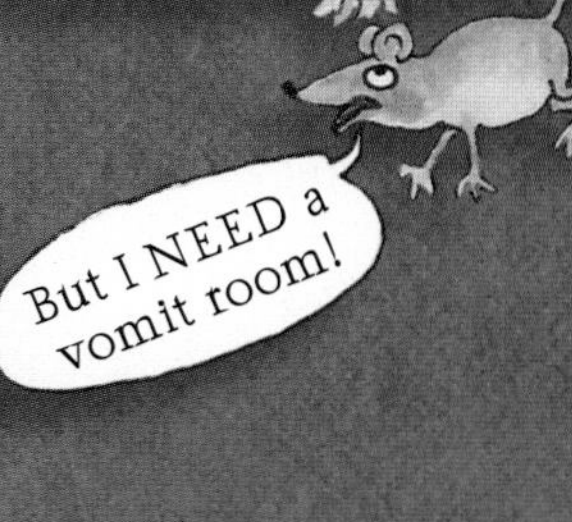
But I NEED a vomit room!

Caligula means "little boots"!

ROMAN EMPERORS – GOOD AND BAD!

Little Boots married and murdered his sister!

Incitatus had a marble stable!

Nero took part in many races and games.

Everyone let him win rather than risk his wrath!

GAIUS AD 37–41
NICKNAMED CALIGULA

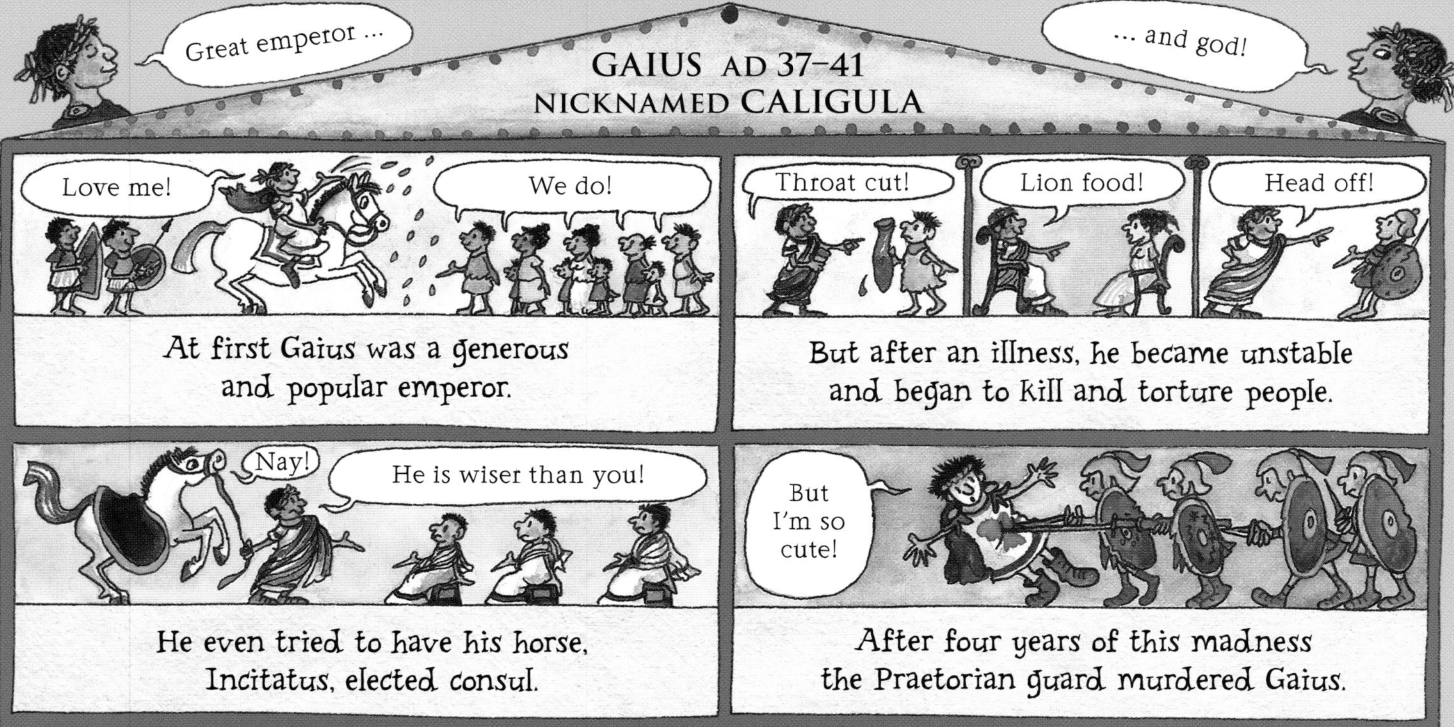

Great emperor ...
... and god!
Love me!
We do!
Throat cut!
Lion food!
Head off!
Nay!
He is wiser than you!
But I'm so cute!

At first Gaius was a generous and popular emperor.

But after an illness, he became unstable and began to kill and torture people.

He even tried to have his horse, Incitatus, elected consul.

After four years of this madness the Praetorian guard murdered Gaius.

NERO
AD 54–68

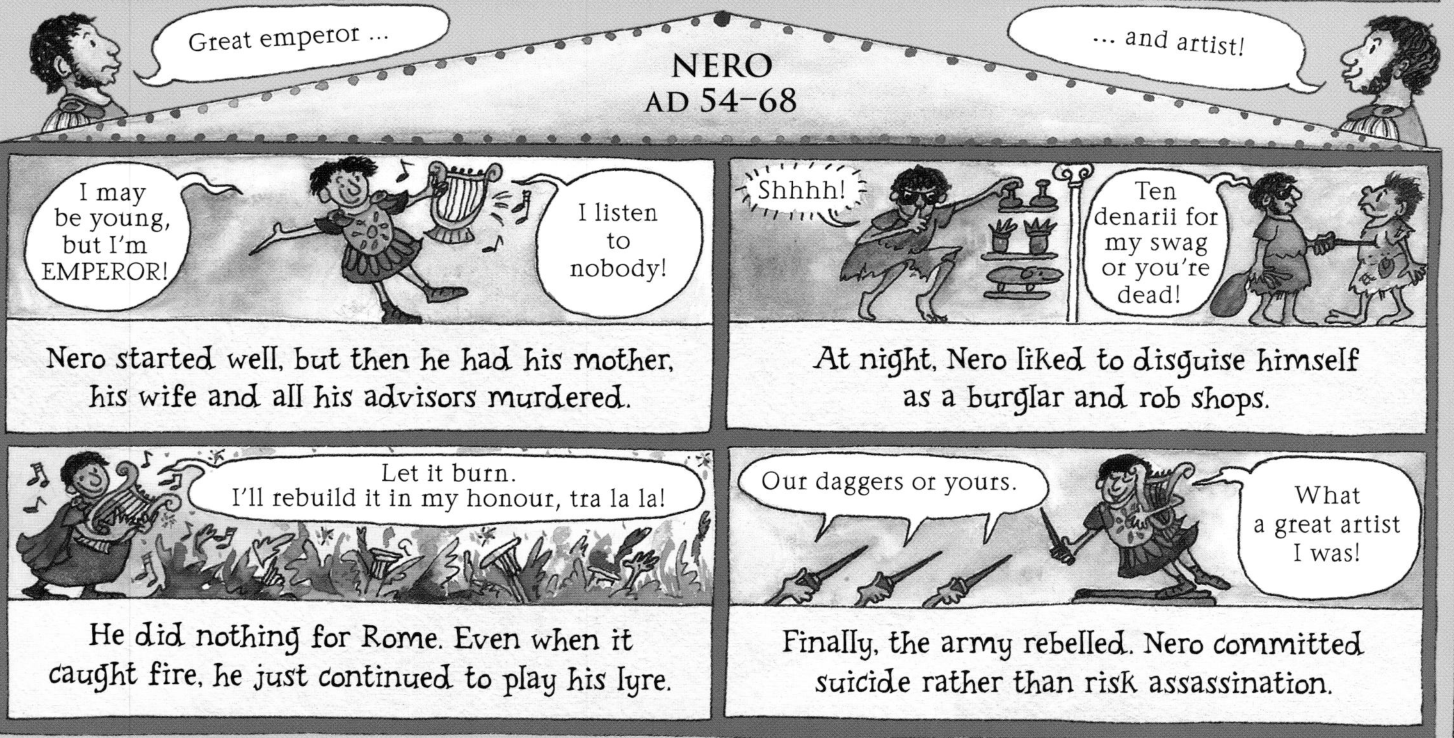

Great emperor ...
... and artist!
I may be young, but I'm EMPEROR!
I listen to nobody!
Shhhh!
Ten denarii for my swag or you're dead!
Let it burn. I'll rebuild it in my honour, tra la la!
Our daggers or yours.
What a great artist I was!

Nero started well, but then he had his mother, his wife and all his advisors murdered.

At night, Nero liked to disguise himself as a burglar and rob shops.

He did nothing for Rome. Even when it caught fire, he just continued to play his lyre.

Finally, the army rebelled. Nero committed suicide rather than risk assassination.

Rome, the little city founded by Romulus, now controlled an empire that stretched across half the known world. This made the Roman emperor the most powerful man in the world – but his job was almost impossible. Under the rule of great emperors, like Augustus, the Empire flourished, but not all emperors were as honourable or as clever.

RES VERA

Nero played music for hours at a time and performed in plays. If his audience left before he had finished they were usually killed.

Vespasian was a general whose legions chose him as emperor!

Great emperor ...

... and general!

TITUS FLAVIUS VESPASIAN
AD 69–79

Let us not be rogues, but scholars and artists!
Hail, Vespasian!

After several useless emperors, Vespasian brought order to Rome.

Out of this rubble will grow the Colosseum!
Wow!

He rebuilt parts of the city still lying destroyed by fire. He even helped clear the rubble.

And you lot are banished!

Vespasian removed the corrupt from power and encouraged the good.

Methinks I am deifying!
An emperor dies standing!

He was one of the few emperors who wasn't poisoned or assassinated.

Vespasian was considered a very jovial host.

He died of a nasty bout of diarrhoea!

Modest emperor ...

... modest man!

MARCUS ULPIUS TRAJAN
AD 98–117

You give me the right to rule.
Hail, Trajan!

Trajan entered Rome on foot, embraced the senators and walked among the people.

No one'll starve on my watch!
Thanks, Trajan.

He cared for the poor and gave his own money to children in need.

Dacia is ours!
Build a victory column!

He was a great emperor and general. He expanded the Empire to its largest extent.

I think I've been poisoned.
You were a star emperor.

Trajan's rule brought glory to the Empire and Rome mourned his death.

Trajan was popular with the people and the Senate!

His ashes were laid in a victory column.

Some emperors were mad, bad and dangerous. Other emperors cared more about wealth and power than the Empire and its people. Bad emperors were to be feared, but a good emperor, along with his family, would be honoured and loved by the Roman people. An emperor was not thought of as a god, but the Senate could deify him (pronounce him a god) after his death.

RES VERA

The Senate prayed for new emperors to be "More fortunate than Augustus and better than Trajan".

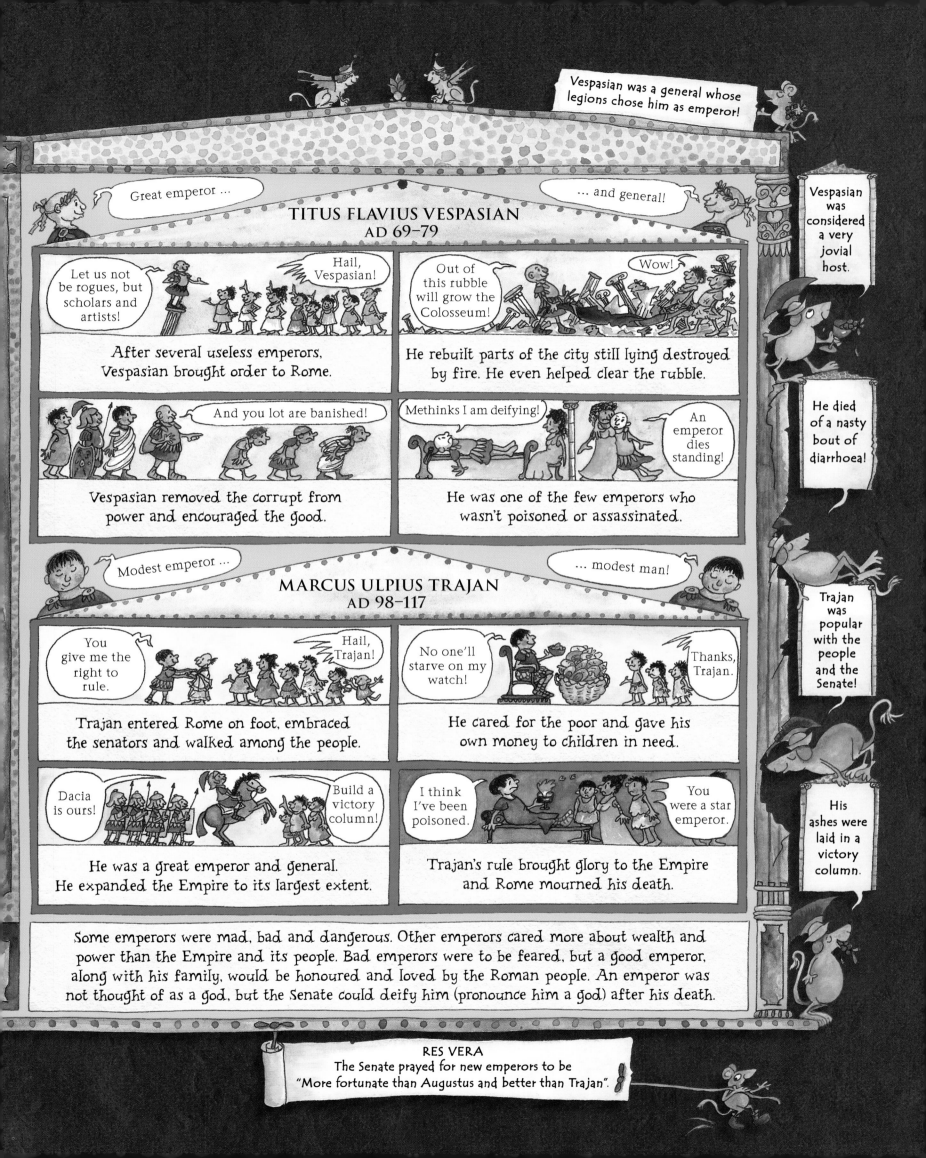

These were scary times for dormice.

THE FALL OF ROME

Between AD 235–284, there was military anarchy.

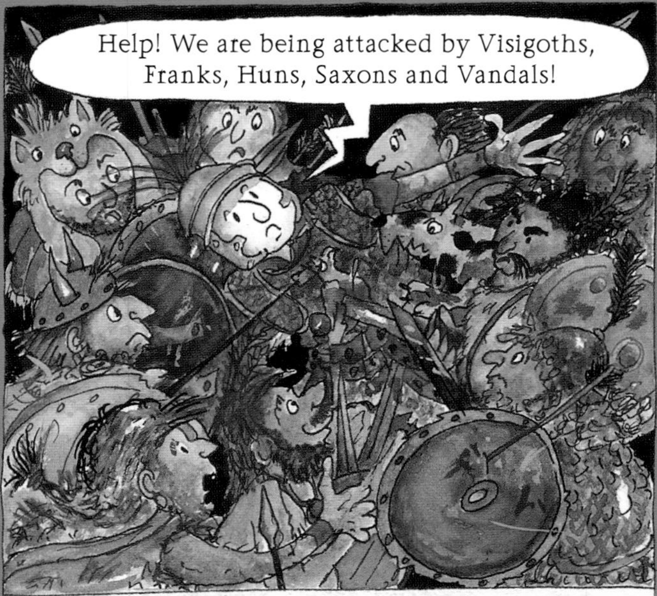

Help! We are being attacked by Visigoths, Franks, Huns, Saxons and Vandals!

Even strong emperors struggled to control the many miles of borders left by Trajan.

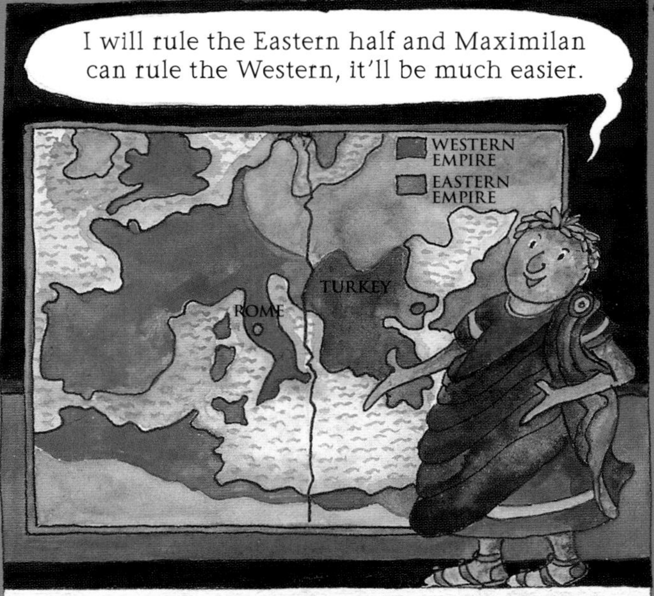

I will rule the Eastern half and Maximilan can rule the Western, it'll be much easier.
WESTERN EMPIRE
EASTERN EMPIRE
TURKEY
ROME

In AD 286, after years of chaos, Emperor Diocletian split the Empire into two parts.

Generals disputed the rule of emperors.

Barbarians were gathering in strength!

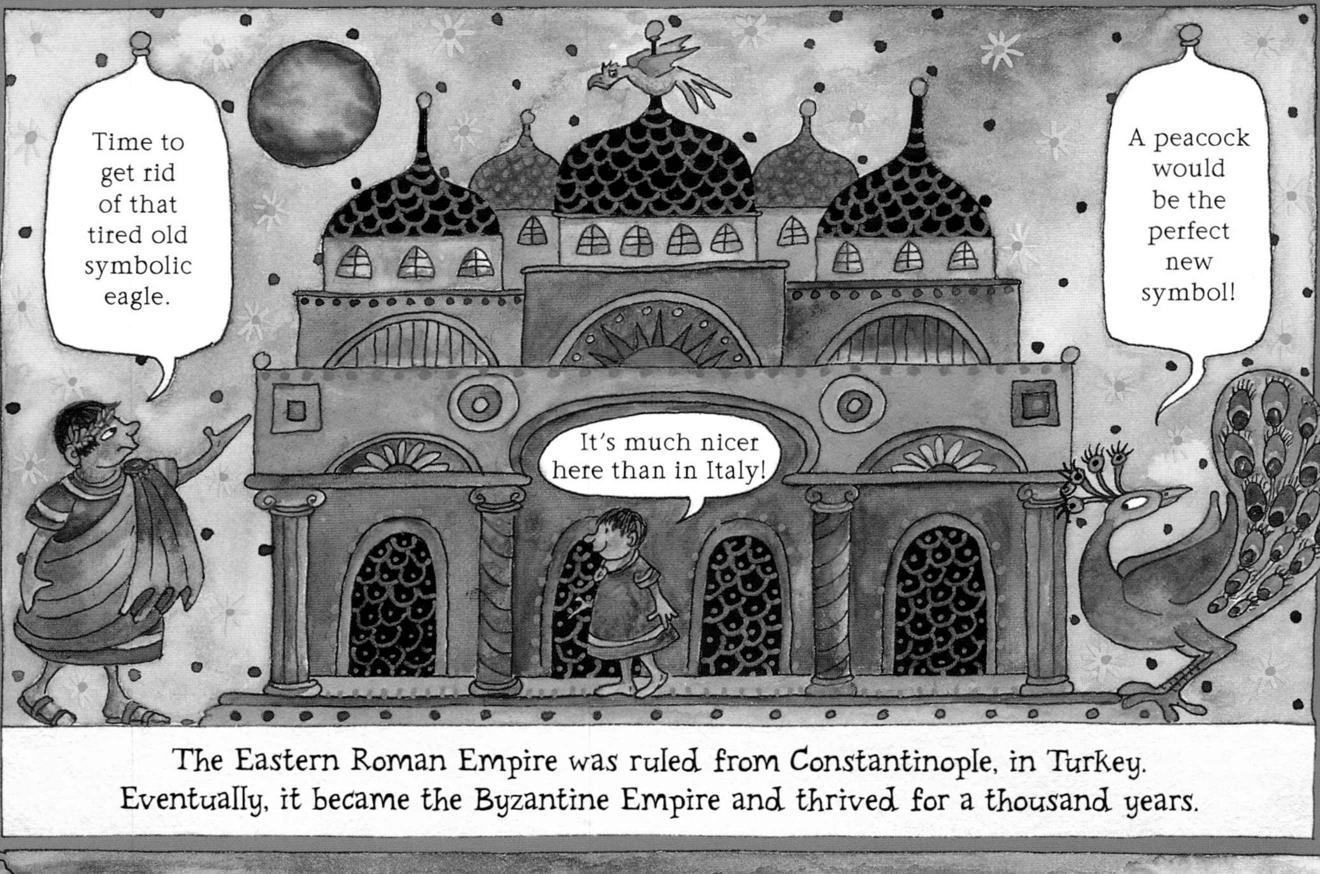

Time to get rid of that tired old symbolic eagle.
A peacock would be the perfect new symbol!
It's much nicer here than in Italy!

The Eastern Roman Empire was ruled from Constantinople, in Turkey. Eventually, it became the Byzantine Empire and thrived for a thousand years.

Splitting the Empire worked until Diocletian retired.

RES VERA

Diocletian persecuted Christians and declared that they must sacrifice to the traditional Roman gods.

THE WESTERN ROMAN EMPIRE

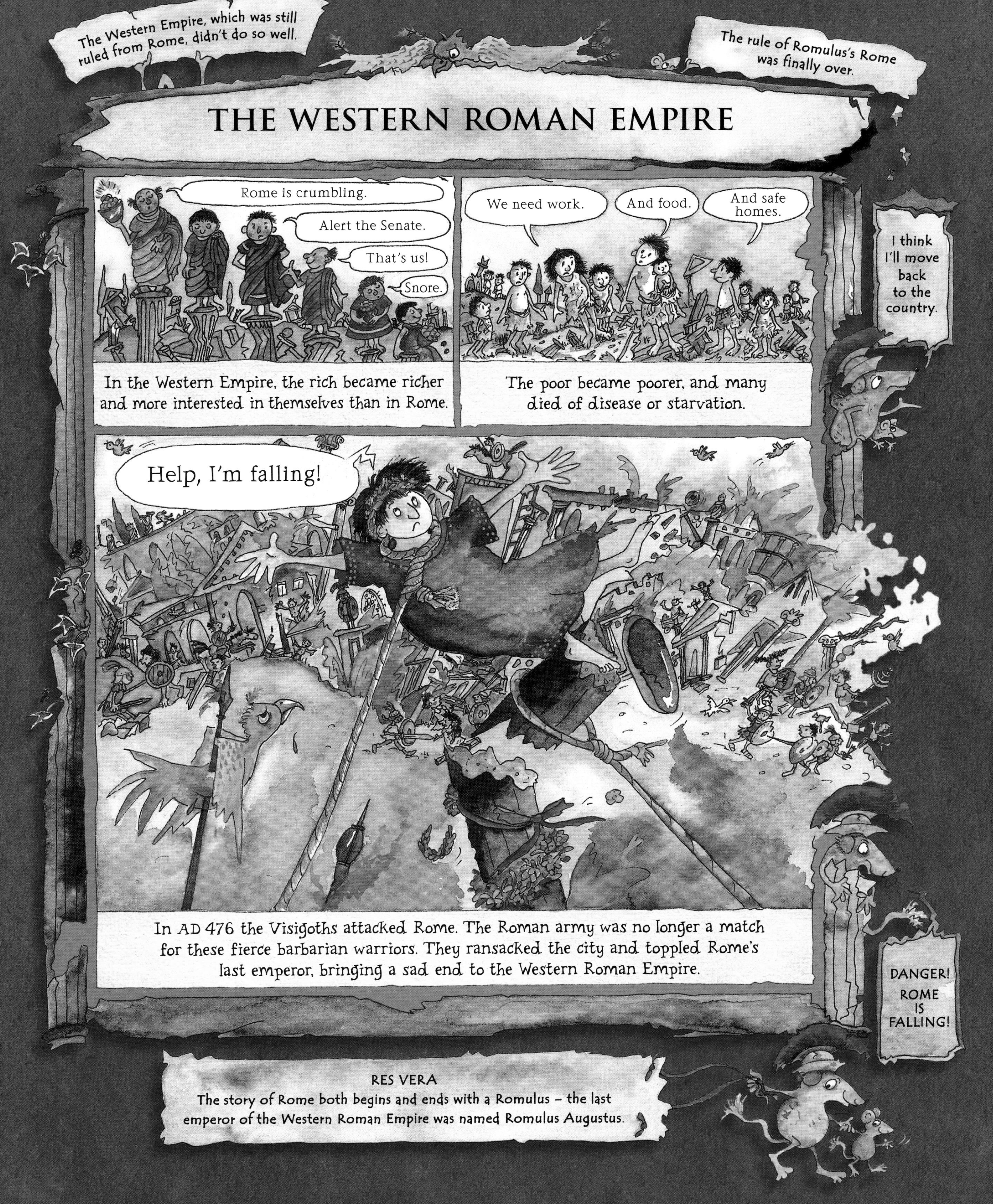
The Western Empire, which was still ruled from Rome, didn't do so well.
The rule of Romulus's Rome was finally over.
THE WESTERN ROMAN EMPIRE
Rome is crumbling.
Alert the Senate.
That's us!
Snore.
In the Western Empire, the rich became richer and more interested in themselves than in Rome.
We need work.
And food.
And safe homes.
The poor became poorer, and many died of disease or starvation.
I think I'll move back to the country.
Help, I'm falling!
In AD 476 the Visigoths attacked Rome. The Roman army was no longer a match for these fierce barbarian warriors. They ransacked the city and toppled Rome's last emperor, bringing a sad end to the Western Roman Empire.
DANGER! ROME IS FALLING!
RES VERA
The story of Rome both begins and ends with a Romulus – the last emperor of the Western Roman Empire was named Romulus Augustus.

First published 2013 by Walker Books Ltd

87 Vauxhall Walk, London SE11 5HJ

This edition published 2014

2 4 6 8 10 9 7 5 3 1

© 2013 Marcia Williams

The moral rights of the author/illustrator have been asserted

This book has been typeset in Godlike, Alpha, Trajan and Tempus

Printed in China

All rights reserved

British Library Cataloguing in Publication Data is available

ISBN 978-1-4063-5455-3

www.walker.co.uk

www.marciawilliams.co.uk

Nunc est stertendum.
Ave atque val —
ZZZZZZZ

MARCIA WILLIAMS

With her distinctive cartoon-strip style, lively text and brilliant wit, Marcia Williams brings to life some of the world's all-time favourite stories and some colourful historical characters. Her hilarious retellings and clever observations will have children laughing out loud and coming back for more!

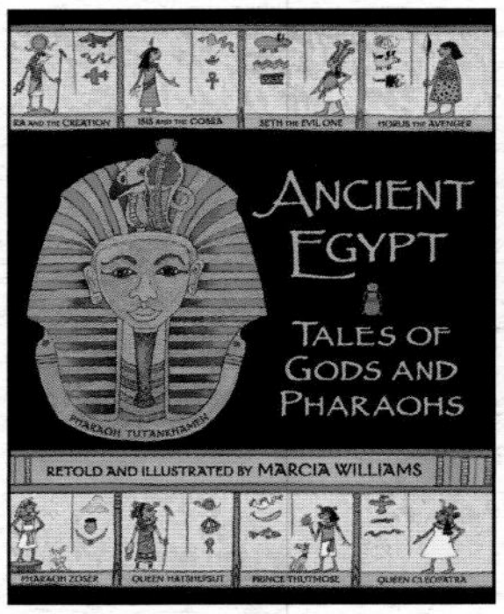
Ancient Egypt
Tales of Gods and Pharaohs
Retold and illustrated by Marcia Williams

ISBN 978-1-4063-3832-4

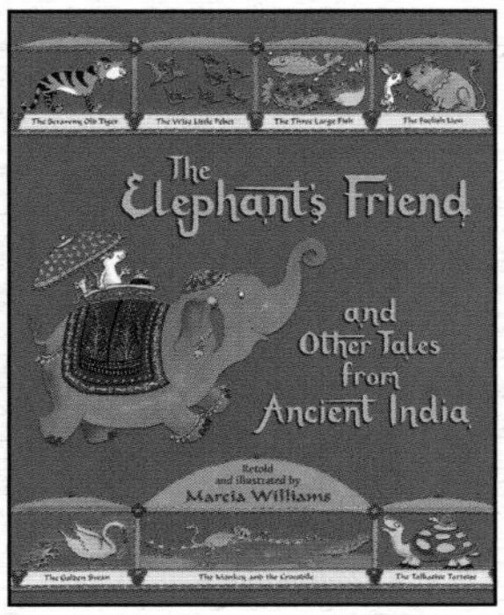
The Elephant's Friend
and Other Tales from Ancient India
Marcia Williams

ISBN 978-1-4063-4492-9

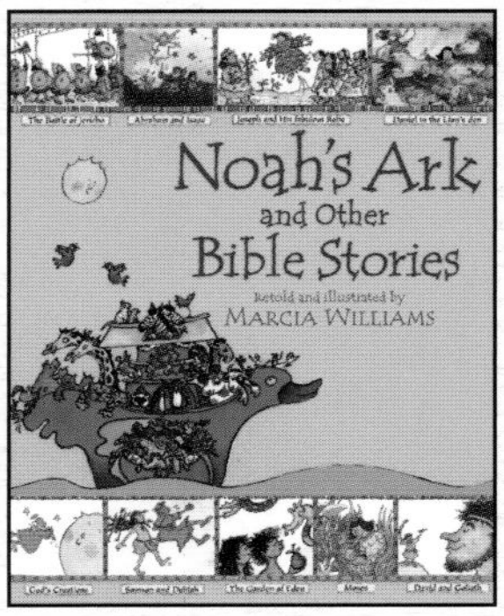
Noah's Ark
and Other
Bible Stories
Marcia Williams

ISBN 978-1-4063-2610-9

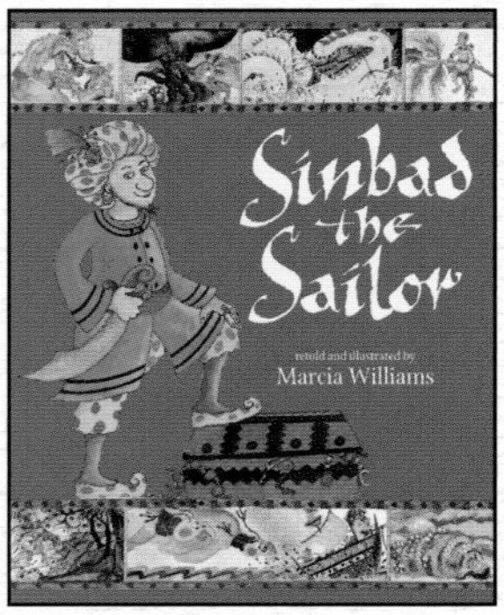
Sinbad the Sailor
Marcia Williams

ISBN 978-1-4063-1944-6

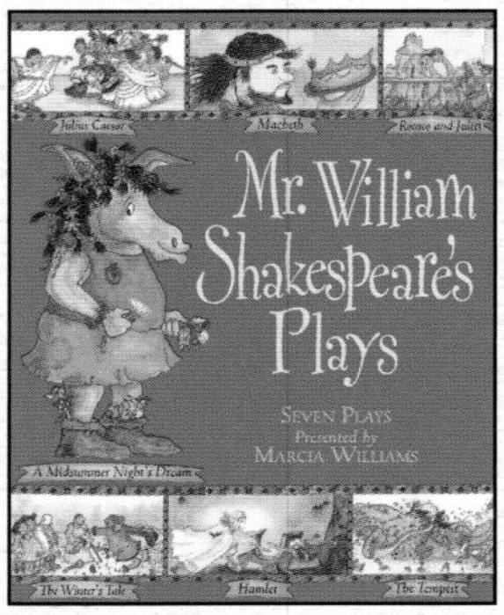
Mr. William Shakespeare's Plays
Seven Plays
Presented by
Marcia Williams

ISBN 978-1-4063-2334-4

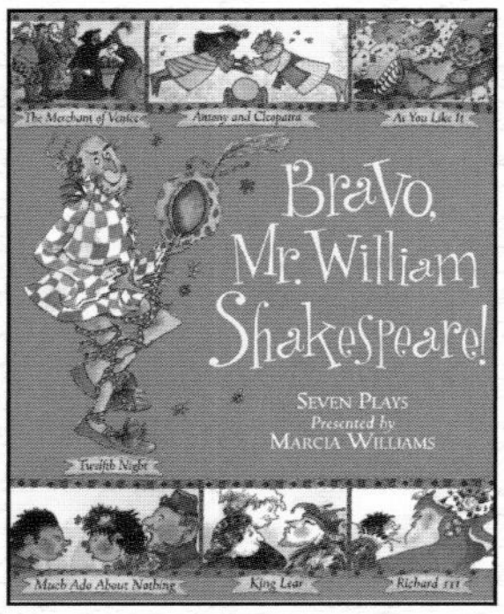
Bravo, Mr. William Shakespeare!
Seven Plays
Presented by
Marcia Williams

ISBN 978-1-4063-2335-1

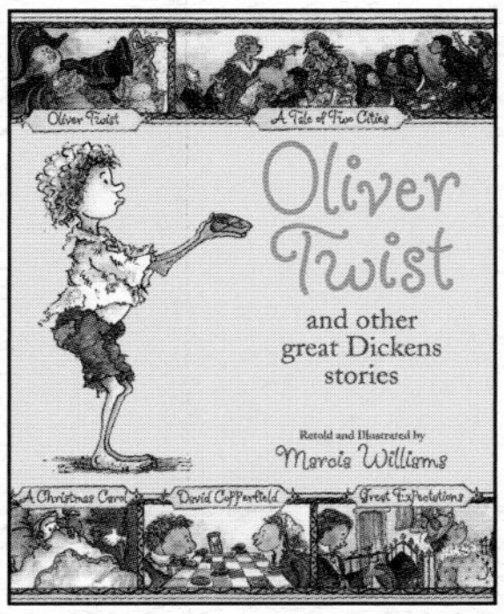
Oliver Twist
and other great Dickens stories
Retold and Illustrated by
Marcia Williams

ISBN 978-1-4063-0563-0

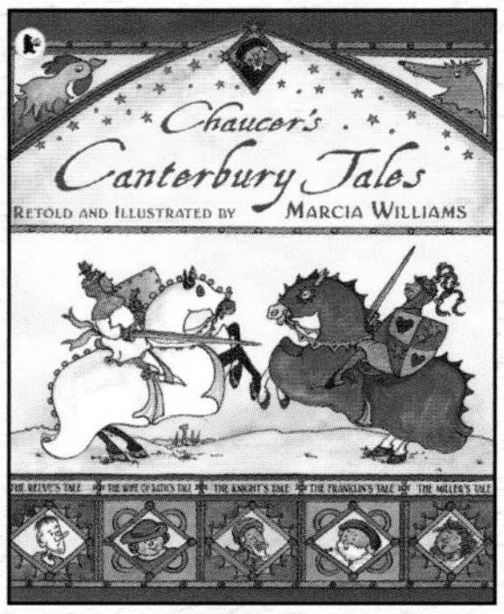
Chaucer's Canterbury Tales
Retold and Illustrated by
Marcia Williams

ISBN 978-1-4063-0562-3

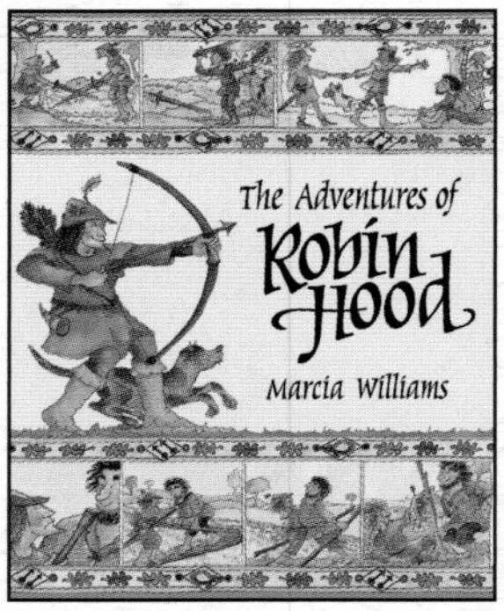
The Adventures of
Robin Hood
Marcia Williams

ISBN 978-1-4063-1137-2

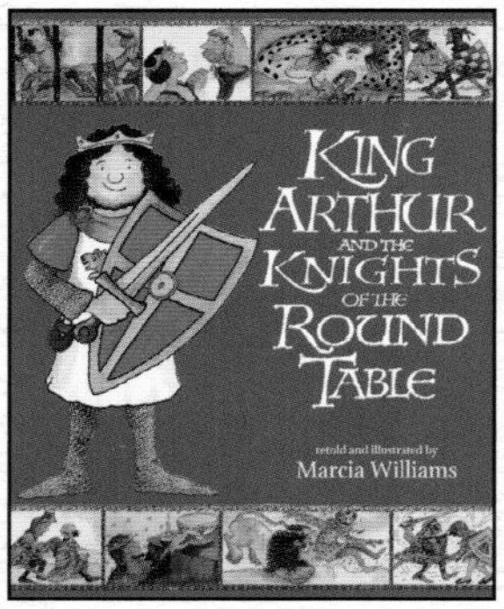
King Arthur and the Knights of the Round Table
Marcia Williams

ISBN 978-1-4063-1866-1

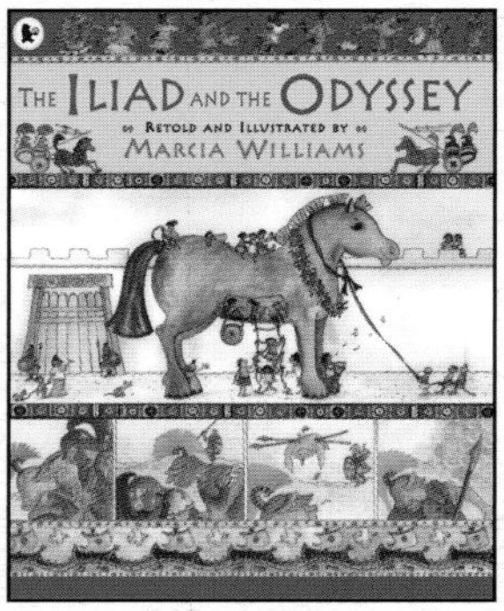
The Iliad and the Odyssey
Retold and Illustrated by
Marcia Williams

ISBN 978-1-4063-0348-3

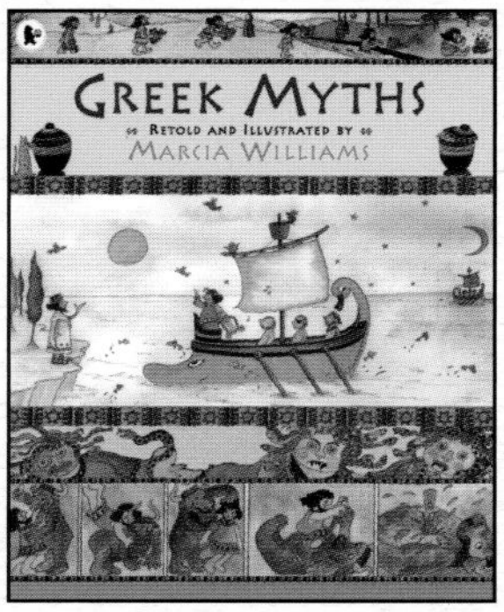
Greek Myths
Retold and Illustrated by
Marcia Williams

ISBN 978-1-4063-0347-6

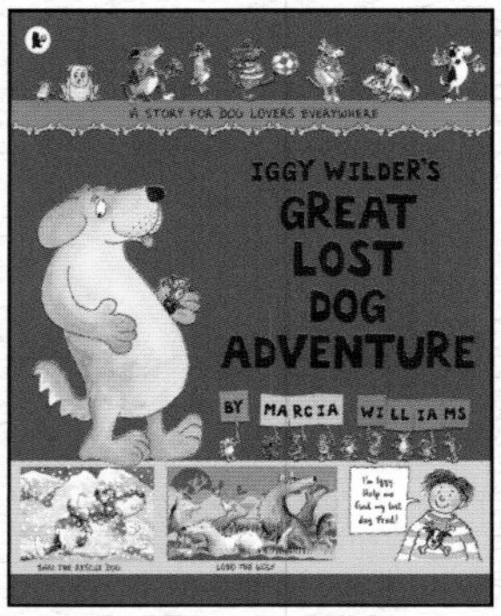
Iggy Wilder's
Great Lost Dog Adventure
By Marcia Williams

ISBN 978-1-4063-2997-1

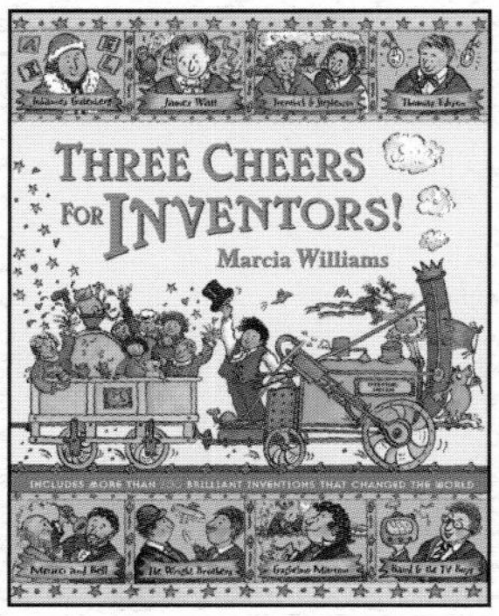
Three Cheers for Inventors!
Marcia Williams

ISBN 978-1-4063-0171-7

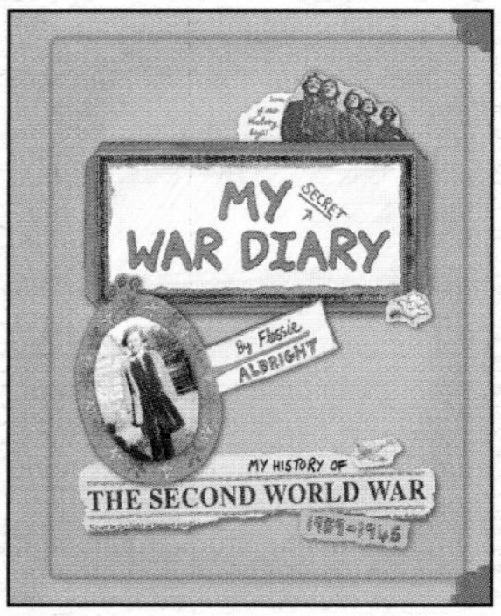
My Secret War Diary
By Flossie Albright
My History of
The Second World War

ISBN 978-1-4063-0940-9

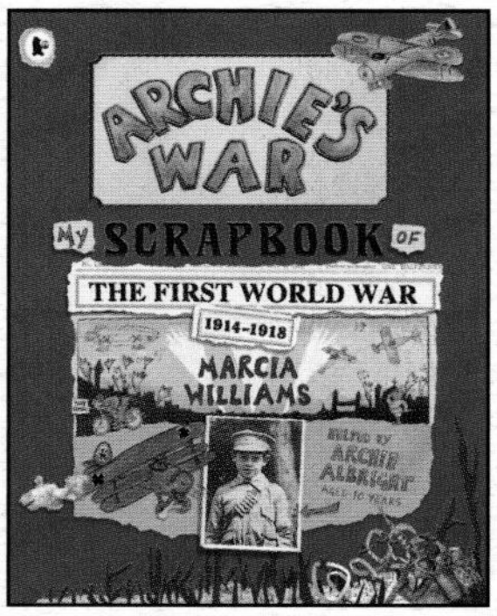
Archie's War
My Scrapbook of
The First World War
1914–1918
Marcia Williams

ISBN 978-1-4063-5268-9

Available from all good booksellers

www.walker.co.uk